TWEET

David Kedson

This is a work of fiction. Names, characters, places, and incidents are either the product of the author's imagination or are used fictitiously, and any resemblance to actual persons (even persons you *wish* were fictional), living or dead, business establishments, events, or locales, is entirely coincidental. Except for Mikhail the Russian sword swallower. He's real.

Cover design and illustrations by Jessica Jaffe © 2017

Contact info:
Please send all communications to: davidkedson@gmail.com
Or visit: http://www.davidkedson.com

One

The mood behind the stage on which President Edward N. Passant would soon speak to the adoring masses could best be described as tense. The tension arose primarily from the fact that the President and his advisors had yet to arrive upon a mutually agreeable subject matter.

The President waved a sheaf of papers in his chief of staff's face. "This is a rally. Whose bright idea was it to talk about *policy?*"

White House Chief of Staff Stanton Young took a deep breath. He centered himself, let calm wash over him. From his years on Wall Street, he'd earned the reputation of having somewhat of a temper, but if the eight months of the Passant Administration had taught him anything it was the need for balance. Fortunately, he'd meditated earlier that day.

"It was my idea, Mr. President," he said. "I thought since this is the kickoff of *Thank You Tour III, the Sequel*, we might want to talk less about how we won the election and more about how we're going to run the country."

"Listen to that crowd." The President gestured toward the area in front of the stage. He beamed as the communal voice crescendoed.

"BUILD THE WALL! BUILD THE WALL!"

"You know what they came for, I know what they came for, and *they* know what they came for. What do you think will happen if I start speaking in specifics?"

He brandished the printed speech again. "And even if I wanted to talk about policy, why the hell would anyone be interested in Yellowstone or Yosemite? Who thought of that one?"

Stanton inhaled again, held it, then exhaled, employing a breathing technique his yoga instructor had taught him. "We've been getting a lot of pushback since your tweet about reducing the national debt by selling the National Park system to ExxonMobil. Cindy and the gang at Interior thought this language might help us get on top of the issue."

The President stared. "Let me give you a free piece of job advice, Stanton. *Never* bring me ideas from staffers who're bleeding out of their whatever."

He reached into his jacket pocket, pulled out his phone.

Stanton jumped forward, all calm and balance forgotten. "Mr. President, *please*. Don't tweet that."

President Passant slipped his phone back into his pocket. "No time, anyway. I have to go out and speak to the People." He crumpled the suggested speech into a ball and tossed it at a trash can. It missed.

"Mr. President, wait. What do you plan to talk about?"

"Don't worry, Stanton. Everyone knows I'm at my best when I'm off-prompter."

Stanton's eyes bugged out. He flattened his voice, a trick he'd learned to keep himself from screaming at inopportune moments.

"I'm not sure that's the best plan, Mr. President."

The President chuckled. He walked toward the stage, past the press pen filled with actors so the crowd would have an appropriate target at which to direct their taunts and frothing-at-the-mouth. He called back over his shoulder.

"Play the song."

The music blared. Another song they'd used without permission from the artist. When the artist had complained on Twitter, the President's response had been to play it again at the next rally. And again, and again. Now he called it his theme song.

I'm coming up so you better get this party started…

The President climbed onto the stage. He raised both thumbs in the air. Over the PA system, the announcer's shouts filled the stadium.

"And now, here he is — savvy billionaire, President of the United States of America, TIME Magazine's Man of the Year, and top-rated host of *The Celebrity Animal Trainer*, now syndicated in fifty-two countries! Please welcome your very own, President Edward N. Passant!"

The crowd went wild. The President signaled for the music to cut off. He raised both thumbs again. "The liberal elites don't like that I'm here talking to you. You tell me, what do we have to say to them?"

"WE WON! WE WON! WE WON!"

The President basked in the adulation. Stanton could see it lift him, could see the next topic moving unfiltered from thought to utterance. "Here's something I bet you didn't know. France has the highest percentage of Muslims in Europe. Can you believe it? *France!* That's what comes from having an open immigration policy."

The crowd roared. A staffer near Stanton whispered to the person next to her. "Highest percentage, really? What about Russia and Turkey, and all those Balkan countries?"

"Forget it, he's rolling."

"We ought to think about blocking immigration from France to the United States. It's something I have to seriously mull over," the President said. "I'm hearing that ISIS is moving its headquarters to a boulangerie in the French Riviera. The generals say no, it isn't happening, but don't listen to the generals, OK? These are the same guys who brought us the Gulf War. And I don't have to tell you what a disaster that was, I was against it from the start. The generals don't know anything. *I'm* the only person who knows our true strategy. I'm the only one who can fix it. Believe me, ISIS is playing right into our hands. If they try to bake one twisted croissant, we're going to *own* their ass."

The cheers rose in pitch and volume, to the point where Stanton had to cover his ears. The President looked back over his shoulder, straight at Stanton. A smirk came over his face. He winked and turned back to the crowd.

"You know what else the lying media says?" He pointed at the fake press pen and the crowd jeered on cue. "They say I don't like our National Parks. Trust me, nothing could be further from the truth. I love National Parks. Nobody loves our National Parks more than I do."

He leaned on the podium. "But I will say I'm going to have to take a hard look at Yellowstone. I mean, something's going on there, most people agree. They're saying Old Faithful may not be so faithful after all. Like maybe it's having an affair... with an illegal geyser from *Mexico*!"

"BUILD THE WALL! BUILD THE WALL!"

The crowd went on for five or ten minutes. Stanton Young covered his face with his hands.

Two

"You brought out your queen too early."

Paul Urbina-Pedisich turned to look at his best friend Artie. "Did not."

The boys were walking the halls of Lower Merion High School, in suburban Philadelphia. It was the start of what school administrators called "lunch-and-learn," a period almost as inaptly named as "study hall," which Paul and Artie had just completed, during which they had as usual eschewed studying in favor of privately poking fun at their fellow students' hairstyles, playing a couple games of internet chess, and snickering at a website comprised entirely of pictures of cats that looked like Hitler.

"I'm not sure it's even up for debate," Artie said. "If your queen hadn't been out so early, the dude wouldn't have been able to take it with his bishop."

"Should've been fine," Paul muttered. "If he hadn't made that damn *en passant* move, I would have had checkmate two moves later. I just didn't notice that when he took my pawn like that it left my queen vulnerable."

"That's another thing. We learned *en passant* in, like, the fifth grade, but I've never seen you use it in a game. Maybe if you did it once in a while you'd recognize it when it's biting you in the butt."

"Shut up, Artie."

They sat on a plastic-covered couch in the vestibule outside the language lab. Same place they'd sat every lunch-and-learn for the first two weeks of the school year. Paul removed his lunchbox from his backpack. Artie dipped his hand into a rumpled paper bag from Au Bon Pain.

"Where'd you get that?" Paul said.

"Mom drove me to school today. We picked it up on the way." Artie removed a tiny loaf of French bread and held it up to the light. Paul breathed in the doughy aroma, rummaged through his lunchbox, looking for anything he might be able to trade.

A group of students walked by. One of them, a very short and very skinny girl named Sylvia, waved as she passed. Dimples filled her cheeks when she smiled. "Hi, Paul."

Paul's lunchbox slipped off his lap. It clattered to the floor. His face turned bright red.

"Dude," Artie said. "She was waving at *me*."

"Did you hear her? She said, 'Paul.'"

'Yeah, I think she has our names reversed."

"Shut up, Artie."

"What's the big deal, anyway?" Artie said. "I mean, she's shorter than you, which admittedly isn't easy, and she's pretty good-looking, but she's not a total babe or anything."

"Have you looked at me recently?"

"Ah." Artie gave a slow nod. "I get it. She's not entirely unattainable but she's enough out of your league to make your unrequited longing worthwhile. Solid logic, dude."

Paul's retort was interrupted by a deep, sneering voice. "Hey, you're in our seats."

Two tall, thick-bodied jocks closed in on them. Not tall enough to be basketball players, or wide enough for football. Probably wrestling or lacrosse, or some sport where they hit each other over the head with mallets.

"Beat it," the taller one said. "These seats are reserved for seniors. Freshmen have to sit on the floor." He pointed to a filthy corner, down by the chemistry classrooms, where the floor tiles looked like somebody'd puked on them.

"We're not freshmen." Paul flinched when the thicker jock faked a punch. "We're sophomores."

The jocks laughed in unison. "Yeah? Prove it. Grow six inches."

Paul stood up. The top of his head came up to the guy's chest. He curled his hand into a fist, measured the distance to the older boy's chin. He twisted his face into the meanest squint he could manage. The jock looked back. He raised one eyebrow.

"OK, we're going," Paul said. He and Artie gathered their things and left. The jocks kept laughing.

"I need to stop by the office, anyway," Artie said. "Got to drop this in the mail."

He waved a postcard. Picture of a greenish alien with a head like an upside-down pear, and the caption, *Greetings from Area 51.* A single sentence was scrawled on the back.

"A letter for my pen pal project for English class," Artie said.

"Weren't you supposed to write, you know, a letter?"

"Technically, Ms. Scully never said how long the letters have to be. She also never said our 'pen pal' had to write back, or even what language we had to use."

"*Technically*, is Pig Latin even a language?"

Artie shrugged. Paul looked at the card again. "Your pen pal project is sending prank postcards to someone famous, isn't it?" Artie shrugged again.

"Stupidest thing I ever heard of," Paul said, though secretly he wished he'd thought of it. His own pen pal was some boring kid named Raul from Marseille, whose letters were written in an indecipherable combination of French, Arabic, and fractured English.

Paul's phone dinged. He dug it out of his backpack. His mouth formed a grimace. "That bastard." He handed his phone to Artie.

"Whoa." Artie looked at the tweet Paul had just received. He quoted it out loud. "'*Didn't you learn en passant in, like, the fifth grade? hahahah I own ur ass!*'"

Paul snatched his phone back. He glanced around for inspiration, found it in the Au Bon Pain bag still clutched in Artie's left hand. He typed furiously with both thumbs.

"Hold it," Artie said. "Let me see it before you send." He grabbed Paul's phone, then rolled his eyes.

"It's a tweet," he said in a tone usually reserved for speaking to toddlers. "You can't spell everything correctly and hope to be taken seriously. Change 'you' to 'u' and 'your' to 'ur.'" He pointed to the first word of the chess term. "And change that to a capital 'N.'"

Paul grumbled but did as he was told. He hit send without further consultation.

Paul U-P

@meltingPUP

U don't own nobody. U couldn't strategize ur way out of a bag of French bread. #UpUrNPassant

11:23 AM - 18 Sep 2017

Artie looked over his shoulder. "The hashtag's a nice touch. Wait, why didn't you hit reply, you know, put the dude's handle in the tweet?" He shook his head. "What's wrong with you? I mean, it's Twitter, not particle physics."

Paul sighed. "Yeah, I'd be better at particle physics."

Three

On Tuesday, the morning after he'd fired the entire Department of the Interior, President Edward N. Passant summoned his chief of staff to the Oval Office. Stanton Young was already on his way. He'd been in his own office since 4am, an hour after the President's latest tweet.

The day he joined the White House communication staff, Stanton had his phone programmed to sound an air raid siren whenever the President accessed Twitter. It meant he hadn't had a full night's sleep in nearly 31 weeks, but especially now that he'd become President Passant's fourth chief of staff in eight months it was almost worth it to get a head start on the day's spin.

This one was a doozie. Stanton had to cancel his primordial sound meditation that morning in favor of damage control. He navigated the White House corridors, perhaps not as centered as he should have been for an Oval Office visit. He paused outside the leader of the free world's door.

Loud music drifted out from under the heavy, slightly curved door, loud enough for Stanton to hear the lyrics.

...when there's nothing to lose and there's nothing to prove, I'm dancing with myself...

Stanton was just a kid during the Eighties, but he recognized this Billy Idol song. He leaned in closer, put his ear against the polished wood, trying to identify the odd tapping and sliding and pounding, reminiscent of Snoopy dancing on top of his doghouse.

Stanton yanked open the door.

The music went silent. President Passant sat behind his desk, breathing just a tad heavily. A single tuft of his orangey hair jutted out of place.

"It's customary to knock, isn't it?" he said.

Stanton stared, mouth open. He watched a couple sheets of paper float down to the floor. Then he remembered his original purpose.

"Mr. President, we've talked about this." He held his phone out in front of him. "You can't go tweeting selfies of you doing tequila shots in a strip club."

"Excuse me," the President said. "Wasn't it you who told me after the geyser thing that I had to show how much I relate to Mexicans?"

Stanton blinked. He was really missing his morning meditation.

The President spread his hands. "Do I have to spell it out for you? Strippers? And *tequila?* Come on."

Stanton stepped to the still-open door. He called to the nearest Secret Service agent. "Do me a favor, please. Find out if there are any reporters or Mexican-Americans — or Latinos of any kind, for that matter — within earshot of the Oval Office, then report back to me. Better make it a thousand-foot radius." He stepped back into the office and closed the door this time. He attempted a smile.

"You asked to see me, Mr. President?"

"Yes. As a matter of fact, I did. I've been thinking."

"That's excellent news, sir."

"No, I mean I've been thinking about my third term."

Stanton began humming his mantra to himself. He couldn't quite remember how it went. He made a mental note to practice it with his instructor. "We're not even a year into our *first* term, sir. Maybe it would be better to focus on—"

"See, that's the difference between *politicians*—" the President sneered the word — "and great businessmen. You don't think ahead."

"Yes, sir," Stanton said. "I'll have my assistant send you a copy of the Constitution. I'll bookmark the Twenty-Second Amendment, which clearly provides that presidents can only serve two terms. We'd need another constitutional amendment to change it."

"Great. Let's do it."

Stanton sighed. "It takes two-thirds of both houses to propose an amendment to the Constitution, sir. Even if every Republican in Congress voted for it, we'd still need fifty Democrats in the House and fifteen in the Senate. And after that, two-thirds of the state legislatures have to approve it. Best case there, we'd be three states short."

The President rapped his fingers on his desk. "I guess we could have Marlena run. The voters would all know I'd still be in control. Or even Prince."

"Your eight-year-old son?"

"He'd be fifteen by the time we'd need him to run. A teenager, not an adult yet, so he'd have to listen to me."

Stanton flopped into a chair. The words "teenager" and "listen," together in the same sentence, had temporarily deprived him of balance.

"Again, we'd need a constitutional amendment, sir," he said from his seat. "Article Two, Section One prohibits foreign-born individuals like your wife or persons below the age of thirty-five, like your youngest son, from serving as President or Vice President."

President Passant ripped his phone from his pocket. Stanton grabbed for his own phone to silence the air raid sound that was surely coming.

 Edward N. Passant

@realEdwardNPassant

Constitution soooo out of touch.
Founding Fathers = Morons!

8:17 AM - 19 Sep 2017

Stanton stood up again, displaying the proper gesture of respect due the President of the United States — even this one. He forced his voice into a serious, sympathetic tone. "I understand your urgency, sir, but with everything else going on, is now really the time to work on something like this?" He put on his best earnest face, held his breath and crossed his fingers behind his back.

"You know what? You're absolutely right. Now's *not* the time." President Passant looked at his watch. "You have one hour. Gather up twelve of our best and brightest and meet me in the Roosevelt Room. That'll be all, Stanton."

The music started again the moment Stanton shut the door behind him.

Four

With the possible exception of the President, who spent most of his time watching cable news, people who worked in the White House tended to be pretty busy, laboring on things like international diplomacy and repealing every executive order and piece of legislation passed by the previous administration. An hour wasn't nearly enough time if your goal was to assemble a crack team of constitutional experts.

Stanton settled on four of his own staffers plus his yoga instructor, who he had a feeling he was going to need. He begged Vice President Panze — who had the uncanny ability to convince the President to listen to reason, occasionally — to attend, along with two of his own aides. He stuck his head inside the White House Counsel's office and dragged out a couple of guys who wore identical suits, identical haircuts, and identical smug expressions, and continually checked their identical watches as if they had somewhere better to be. Which they probably did. Finally, Stanton corralled the Attorney General of the United States, who Stanton had found aimlessly roaming the halls a few minutes earlier.

President Passant sailed into the room, accompanied by music which seemed to come from his inner jacket pocket. Stanton recognized it as the theme music from the President's TV show, *The Celebrity Animal Trainer*, though he'd never seen the show, itself.

The President stood up. He reached into his pocket and the music stopped. "We all know why we're here," he said. "It's going to be cutthroat, it's going to be crazy, it's going to be fun. Even if it isn't, I'm the President so you're all going to do it. It's time to face the music." His hand dipped into his pocket again, and a different set of dramatic chords filled the room. He sat down with a flourish.

"First thing, we'll split you into teams. Let's go with my favorite: man vs. woman just works. So, all the men on one side and all the women on the other."

"Uh, Mr. President," Stanton said. "There's only one woman in the room."

The President glared, but not at Stanton, aiming instead toward where a camera might be if they were actually filming. "Why did you only cast one woman?"

"You gave me an hour, Mr. President. When ninety-two percent of the employees above the level of secretary in the West Wing are white males, what did you expect?"

"No matter. How about lawyers vs. non-lawyers. That's a good one. Give the audience a rooting interest. Everybody hates lawyers."

"Everyone in the room is a lawyer, Mr. President. Except you."

This time he did glare at Stanton. "Even her?" He gestured at the lone woman in the room, who was currently serving as Stanton's press liaison.

"Yes, sir. Women can be lawyers, too."

"You're taking all the fun out of this, Stanton. Just take your own staff and Vice President Panze can have everyone else. Your first tasks are to pick a team project manager and a team name. Meet me back here in twenty minutes."

He rose and swept from the room.

Vice President Panze gave Stanton a hard look. "You got me out of a security briefing for *this*?"

"I'm sorry, Mr. Vice President, but if you can't talk him down from this constitutional amendment nonsense, nobody can. Let's just follow his instructions for now. It's probably for the best. You and your group stay here and my team can confab in my office."

Stanton's assistant chief of staff, whose name was Craig, claimed to be an avid watcher of President Passant's show. Stanton couldn't decide whether to let him lead the conversation or fire him on the spot.

"This part is easy," Craig said. "Obviously, you'll be our project manager, Mr. Young. The team name doesn't really matter, so long as the President doesn't think it's lame. Anybody have an idea?"

After fifteen minutes of lively debate, they chose the name "The Amenders" over "Young Bloods," three votes to two. Stanton abstained from the balloting, wondering instead whether he would have preferred being defenestrated from the 57th floor of Passant Place.

A few minutes later, the President summoned them back to the Roosevelt Room, which he inexplicably called the "Board Room." The Vice President's team had named themselves, "The Panzer Tanks." The Vice President himself appeared ready to spit heavy artillery.

The President had been joined in the room by his son, Edward, Jr., and his daughter, Isabel. He dispensed with the music this time. "OK, here's what's going to happen. Each team must draft a constitutional amendment that will either allow me to run for a third term, or allow someone under my direct and immediate control to run after my two terms are up. Then you're going to lobby your amendment with Congress and the state legislatures. The winner is the team that comes up with the most commitments to vote for your amendment from the House, Senate, and statehouses, combined." He gestured at his children. "Isabel and Edward, Jr., are here to keep an eye on you and also to help. Use their expertise."

"Expertise?" One of Stanton's staffers whispered. "In what, constitutional theory or selling ladies' footwear?"

"Shhh," Stanton said. A few minutes later his team was back in his office.

Stanton took the seat behind his desk and gave his staff a big smile. "The President so rarely asks us to draft legislation. This is a big opportunity for us. So who wants to come up with a constitutional amendment that has next to no chance of passing?"

Craig pulled out a notepad. "Repealing the Twenty-Second Amendment seems like a losing proposition. We won't get any Democrats, for starters. I'm not sure even our friends would be happy allowing President Passant to run for unlimited terms." He tapped his pencil on the nearest tabletop. "Frankly, I think dropping the age restriction might be the easiest to accomplish. They'll have no clue why we want it. It'll look like the kind of meaningless exercise of power people have come to expect from us."

The others agreed. Stanton shook his head. "The key is finding enough bipartisan support. There just aren't enough red states to pull off something like this."

"Oh my God, I've got it," Stephanie, the press liaison, said. "Let's make more states."

The door opened. The President's oldest son, Edward, Jr., whose best-known expertise was telling fat jokes on Howard Stern, invited himself into the room. He sat down without a word, made a motion for Stephanie to continue.

"How many solid red states are there? Thirty?" she said. "Cut them all in half, turn them into two states each. Problem solved."

Stanton was torn between pride that his staff could think so far outside the box and horror that his name might eventually become associated with the idea. It must have shown in his expression, because Stephanie's face flushed. "I know this all sounds crazy, sir, but adding states might be easier than getting the constitutional amendment any other way. All you need to add a new state is a simple majority of both houses. Plus the old state would have to agree if you're creating a new state out its existing territory."

"Would they agree?" another staffer said.

"I don't see why not. They'd essentially get two extra senators, plus the six red states who only have one congressman would get another. Not to mention sixty-six additional red state electoral votes." She tried to meet Stanton's eyes, but he was too busy envisioning the epitaph on his tombstone. "Think about it. We'd never lose a presidential election again."

The room buzzed with excitement. Craig clapped his hands. "Not to mention the boon to flag manufacturers. Just think what this could do for the GDP."

Stanton sighed. "I'm sorry, but I can't support this. Adding thirty states to the Union? Do I even have to say how insane that is? The Dems would go ballistic and you still wouldn't get your constitutional amendment. Even with the six additional friendly representatives, you'd be forty-some votes short in the House. Frankly, I'm not even sure enough Republicans would favor such a blatant attack on democracy. Lose three votes in the Senate and you won't even get your new states. But *everyone* will remember we tried it."

Craig and Stephanie shared a look. Craig bit his lip. "That's a great point, Mr. Young, but I'm not sure we can afford to ignore this idea." He held up one hand. "Please, sir, hear me out. Have you ever *seen* the show? Whoever gets fired from the losing team gets locked in a cage for an hour with a chair, a whip, and a hungry Bengal tiger." He glanced around the room "I can't speak for anyone else, but I just had this suit pressed."

Edward, Jr. laughed, though it was unclear whether his mirth was prompted by events in the room or by his smartphone, on which he was watching members of his hunting lodge live-tweet themselves poaching endangered species. "Have none of you read my father's books? *Think Sneaky? Piss People off like a Billionaire? The Art of the Steal?* Any of them? No wonder you're all clueless. Listen up, people. You don't have to actually make new states, you just have to *threaten* to do it."

Craig's eyes went wide. "Hold the phone, I get it now. We tell the Democrats we'll hold off on wrecking the Republic if they work with us on the presidential age restriction. They'll be so happy we're not going for the new states thing that they'll fall all over themselves to pass our amendment. We'll win every *blue* state as well as most of the red ones." He looked at Stanton. His eyes went large. "This could actually work. Please, sir, give it a chance. None of us want four-foot-long claw marks on our backs."

"Fine." Stanton sagged in his chair. "I'll convey your threat to the Minority Leader and I'll give the Speaker a heads-up."

There was much rejoicing.

Stanton's phone rang. The President, with news of a "new development." Stanton listened for a few seconds. He massaged his temples. "Yes, sir, I understand. Thank you, Mr. President."

He turned to Craig. "New instructions. Someone has to take a copy of this ridiculous amendment we haven't yet drafted and bring it to Georgetown Law where the famous constitutional scholar, Lawrence Vibe, is giving a lecture. Whichever team's amendment Mr. Vibe likes best will get voting commitments from three swing state senators."

One of the junior staffers said, "On it." He left the room and returned a few minutes later carrying an old-fashioned pen and inkwell and what looked like a piece of two hundred-year-old parchment. "I've seen the show, too," he said. "Trust me, he'll like this."

The other staffers got busy on their phones. Stanton made his two calls, as promised. He spent the rest of his time in the corner with his yoga instructor, learning a new aromatherapy technique that might calm his budding ulcers.

Five

Stanton felt the need to fret coming on. Not that he was worried about being locked in a cage with a 475-pound carnivore, but whenever the President got enthusiastic about something, it made Stanton nervous. Especially when he remembered that the President's *third* chief of staff had lasted just a day and a half. They walked back to the Roosevelt Room. His staffers all watched him, picking up on his non-verbal cues. He attempted to find his inner ch'i, use the energy to project a positive, optimistic tranquility over them all.

They reached the room. President Passant sat on one side of the long table, along with his two adult children. He played the music from his pocket again. The remaining twelve people crammed themselves on the other side, each team huddling close together.

"It's the moment of truth," the President said. "It's not going to be pleasant, but that's the way it is. When we're done here, somebody will be fired."

A tiger's roar sounded in the distance. Stanton couldn't tell if it was part of the recording.

"I've received copies of each team's amendments, and I've discussed them with constitutional expert Lawrence Vibe. Personally, I don't know why neither team tried to get me a third term. Seems like the simplest solution to me, but what do I know? I'm just the richest guy in the room and President of the United States." He rubbed his hands together. "Let's start with the Amenders. Your amendment abolishes the age restriction for Presidents and Vice Presidents. That would allow my son Prince to run for President. Stanton, do you think you won?"

Stanton embraced the ch'i. He gave his arm a hearty swing. "You bet, Mr. President."

His energy projection technique apparently needed work. Several of his staffers' faces paled. Their hands trembled visibly. Stephanie began chewing her nails.

The President leaned forward. "Who was your biggest star?"

"They're all stars in my book, sir."

President Passant frowned. Craig looked at the President, then at his boss. He seemed to be visualizing four-foot-long claw marks. "That would have to be Stephanie, Mr. President. She came up with our bargaining chip and she made the most phone calls by far."

The President ogled the only woman on the team side of the table. The corner of his mouth quirked upward. "Old boyfriends?"

"No, sir." Stephanie appeared confused. "I know a lot of the senior staffers on the Hill." She paused a moment. "I guess I did go out on a blind date with one of them, back in law school, but he couldn't take the call this morning. I spoke to his colleague instead."

"Is he rich?" The President leaned further over the table, showing off thousand-dollar cufflinks and a full head of orangey hair that seemed to have a life of its own.

Stephanie shook her head. President Passant's leer widened. "Then he has no chance with *you*, does he? Tell me, does he fly on Air Force One?"

Vice President Manchester Panze slapped the arm of his chair. "Mr. President, please!"

The President swiveled toward his second-in-command. "Fine, let's turn to the Panzer Tanks. Your amendment allows foreign-born citizens to serve as President. That would allow my wife Marlena to run. Do you think *you* won, Manchester?"

"I believe democracy was the big loser today, Mr. President."

President Passant turned to his daughter. "Isabel, how'd the Panzer Tanks do today?"

Isabel Passant consulted a tablet computer. "A strong showing, Mr. President. One-hundred eighty votes in the House, thirty-five in the Senate, and nineteen state legislatures. A total of two-hundred-thirty-four."

The President raised his phone. "I have received a text message from Lawrence Vibe. He has made his decision." He affected a solemn face and waited for the commercial break that wasn't coming. Finally, he smiled. "He has chosen... the Amenders! He felt the Panzer Tanks' amendment might cause unforeseen consequences. Do we want to pass a law that might allow Vladimir Putin to run for President of the United States? I don't want that kind of competition." He smirked at the Vice President. "You should have thought of that, Manchester. Lawrence also liked the packaging of the Amenders' work product. The calligraphy was a nice touch."

Stanton's team all high-fived the junior staffer who'd penned the amendment and was now contemplating witty answers for his soon-to-be-scheduled interview on *Fox and Friends*. The President announced their reward, which was signed commitments from both of Maine's senators and the senior senator from New Hampshire.

"Ooh." Craig consulted his list. "We didn't have him."

Edward, Jr. typed the additions into his iPad. "That brings the Amenders' total to three-hundred-five representatives, sixty-one senators, and seven state legislatures. A total of three-hundred-seventy-three."

The Panzer Tanks gasped as one. Stanton's team had won by almost 140 votes. The President said, "Well done, Amenders. Next week's episode will be about getting this thing passed. You have some work to do in the state legislatures."

He addressed Stanton. "Take your team to celebrate. The Panzer Tanks and I are going to have a little chat. It's a nasty time, but unfortunately that's the way it goes."

Stanton led his staffers from the room. He told them to hold their whoops and high-fives until they were outside the building. Then he loitered in the hallway to watch the rest of the spectacle unfold.

"Well, Manchester, your team did a good job but it wasn't enough," the President said. "Tell me, who was your weakest link?"

The Vice President sat, stony-faced. He said nothing.

"Come on, Manchester. You have to make a decision. Who are you taking back to the Board Room with you?"

The Vice President closed his eyes. "With all due respect, Mr. President, and I don't use this language lightly, but what the fuck are you talking about?"

President Passant rolled his eyes. "You have to choose two from your team and then meet me here in the Board Room. One of the three of you will be fired and must feel the tiger's teeth."

"You've got to be kidding, Mr. President."

"No, Manchester. I'm not."

The two men locked glares across the table. The President removed his jacket and rolled up his sleeves, like he was getting ready to arm wrestle.

"Whatever," the Vice President said. "I'll take the Attorney General and either one of Tweedle Dee and Tweedle Dum over there." He pointed at the two White House lawyers, whose hair was now identically disheveled. "Doesn't matter which."

"That wasn't so hard, was it?" President Passant said. "Now, who deserves to be fired?"

"You don't want me to answer that question, Mr. President."

The President turned to the Attorney General. "Do you think you should be fired, Jeff?"

"No sirree, Bob," the Attorney General drawled. "And I'll tell you why, Mr. President. Right now, you got yourself an A.G. who's against the Civil Rights Act, the Voting Rights Act, and the First, Fourth, Fifth, and Fourteenth Amendments. I've been confirmed by Congress. If y'all had to replace me, think you'd get that lucky again?"

President Passant nodded. "How about you?" he asked the White House Counsel guy.

The lawyer swallowed visibly. "Honestly, sir, and with all due respect to the Vice President, our problem was our project manager. Vice President Panze spent years in Congress. He was a respected governor. He knows *everybody* we needed for this project. But he refused to make a single phone call. I hate to say this, but he just wasn't a team player."

The President frowned. "That true, Manchester?"

Vice President Panze stood up. "While you decided to host a showing of *The Celebrity Constitutional Amender*, I thought it might be a better idea to help head off escalating hostilities on the Turkish/Syrian border."

"I'll take that as a yes," President Passant said. "You leave me no choice, Manchester. You're fi—"

"Stop right there, Mr. President." The Vice President's voice was just above a whisper, but it seemed to sizzle the air above the table. "You can't fire me. I'm the duly elected Vice President of the United States. And I'm done playing your games."

He stalked from the room. He didn't notice Stanton as he shoved him out of his way.

The rest of the Panzer Tanks scurried out after their leader. President Passant watched them go. He reached behind him, picked up the receiver from a White House phone sitting on a solid oak credenza, eyes never leaving the doorway through which the Vice President had just stormed out. "*Nobody* tells me what I can and cannot do."

Into the receiver, he said, "Get me Stew Cannon." A few seconds later, he said, "Stew, you're my chief strategist, and right now I need some strategizing."

He drew the receiver closer and huddled around it. Stanton had to strain to hear him.

"We have to fire the Vice President."

Six

When the top brass filed in to the big conference room at Langley, Seamus Callahan knew who and what was going to be the topic of discussion. He hadn't risen to the level of a CIA specialized skills officer by being stupid.

He had only a vague recollection of the incident. He supposed his condition was getting worse. He'd had the Supreme Leader of North Korea in his sights, and the next thing he knew he'd woken up in a cargo container on a merchant marine vessel bound for the Lesser Antilles. His superiors at the CIA hadn't been thrilled with his job performance.

At his desk, Seamus closed his computer screen, which had displayed a memo about the recent dearth of croissant sales in the flyover states, in the wake of the President's latest speech. He wondered why anybody at the CIA cared enough to write such a memo. He wondered whether anyone in any of those states had ever eaten a croissant before. He plugged in his earphones and pretended to be listening to a mission briefing, while in fact he was hearing the banal greetings being exchanged inside the conference room. He certainly hadn't risen to the level of specialized skills officer without knowing how to plant an eavesdropping device.

The assistant director of the National Clandestine Service cleared his throat. He was Seamus's boss's boss, pretty high up the totem pole for something like this, but Seamus supposed that's how seriously the Agency was taking the incident. "Let's get this over with," he said. "How does a CIA assassin fall asleep in the middle of a critical operation?"

"He's been diagnosed with narcolepsy," Seamus's boss said. "He couldn't help it."

"Excuse me?" the assistant director said. "Are you telling me we hired someone who uncontrollably falls asleep at unpredictable times as an *assassin*?"

"Of course not, sir. Apparently, the condition doesn't usually manifest itself until a person is fifteen to thirty years old. Callahan's twenty-eight. He was only diagnosed recently. Before that he was one of our best."

That was true. In fact, his first incident had been at a little party his office-mates had thrown in honor of his winning CIA employee-of-the-month for the third consecutive month. They all thought it was hilarious, that he'd passed out because he'd had too much to drink. He'd woken up at his desk outfitted in a hula skirt and strategically placed coconut shells. The second time had been at a press conference, sitting on stage while the President of the United States spoke. Seamus had caused a ruckus when he unceremoniously flopped out of his chair. The President made some mordant remark about it. The video topped Jimmy Fallon's top ten list.

Since then, the episodes had increased in frequency, but he hadn't had one on the job until that night in North Korea.

"I don't care about his past performance," the assistant director said. "He has to go. Have him clean out his desk this afternoon."

Seamus clutched the edge of his desk. His skills weren't easily transferable to the private sector, unless he wanted to work for an unscrupulous organization like the Cosa Nostra, or Facebook.

"You can't fire him," an unfamiliar female voice said.

After several seconds of silence, the assistant director said, "You're from Human Resources?"

"That's right, and you can't terminate somebody just because he has a disability. Have you never heard of the Americans with Disabilities Act? You have to make reasonable accommodations that make it possible for him to perform his job duties."

"As an assassin? Are you kidding me? How could he possibly perform those job duties?"

"Then find him a new job. He's disabled, not incompetent. Make him an analyst, put him behind a desk. We're part of the United States bureaucracy. You can't fire the guy unless you catch him engaged in illegal or morally reprehensible conduct."

Another voice Seamus didn't recognize spoke up. "Illegal or immoral? Like shooting someone?"

"Use your head," the assistant director said. "We can't go down *that* slippery slope. None of us would have jobs."

The bigwigs kept talking. Seamus's hands began to relax. He could tell by their tone that he would maintain his employment in some form or other. The tension flowed out of his body.

Next thing he knew, he was face-down on his desk and the top brass were leaving the building.

Seven

Paul Urbina-Pedisich sat in his AP biology class, ogling an octopus named Orville. Paul's teacher, Mr. Harrison, said octopuses were among the most intelligent creatures on Earth, that they could learn, process complex information in their heads, and behave in clever and unpredictable ways. Paul wondered if Orville the Octopus was so smart, then why was it living in a murky aquarium in the back of a biology lab and not in the penthouse suite in Passant Place. Then Paul considered who actually did live in the penthouse suite in Passant Place and figured maybe he'd answered his own question.

Still, when Mr. Harrison announced he needed volunteers to study and help take care of the octopus, Paul's hand shot up. About twenty other hands went up as well, but after Mr. Harrison explained that the assignment involved spending valuable after-school time, and was not an opportunity to goof off *during* school, the only arms that remained in the air were Paul's, Artie's, and Sylvia's, the skinny girl who had once waved to Paul during lunch-and-learn.

Soon after the final bell rang that day, the three youngsters gathered around Orville, waiting for Mr. Harrison to tell them what to do.

The teacher entered the lab from a back room. "Ah, excellent," he said. "Thank you for volunteering to help our school's octopus. Basically, I'd like you to do two things for me. First, I need someone to feed him. Octopuses are very picky about what they eat. Some will only eat live shellfish. Luckily, Orville has taken a liking to frozen shrimp. We have a whole bucket in a freezer in the back room." He pointed at the door through which he'd come.

"Frozen shrimp?" Artie said. "We're not supposed to give him any cocktail sauce, though, right?"

Mr. Harrison gave an I-could-be-making-triple-my-salary-at-some-biotech-startup smile. "Good call, Artie. The second thing I need you to do is in some ways even more important. Octopuses need mental stimulation, and Orville's environment is necessarily limited by the size of his tank. I'd like you to change his toys every few days, and—"

"Toys?" Sylvia said. "Like dolls and action figures?"

"Are you kidding? Dolls?" Artie said. "Orville is a *boy* octopus."

Sylvia's eyes narrowed. She flexed her fingers. "Are you saying dolls aren't good enough for boys? I suppose *you* want to give him a football?"

She began her advance. She was at least six inches shorter than Artie, but her nails sure looked sharp. Artie chewed his lip but stood his ground. Paul would have stepped between them, except he knew from TV sitcoms that the well-meaning friend who got caught in the middle was almost always the one who got hurt.

Fortunately, Mr. Harrison intervened. "Orville would enjoy both dolls and small rubber footballs. Any toy, really, so long as it doesn't have small parts that would present a swallowing hazard. If you want a little fun, put some food inside a jar and watch him unscrew the top."

He pointed at an old-style telegraph device. "OK, last thing. Octopuses generally communicate by changing the shape and color of their bodies. But I've been trying to teach Orville a few simple words in Morse code, to see if we can communicate linguistically. Maybe you three can continue that experiment."

"Wait, I know," Artie said. "We could open a Twitter account, ask Orville questions, and then tweet what he says."

This time, Mr. Harrison's smile seemed more genuine. "Great idea, Artie. I can see this project is in good hands. I've already fed Orville today, so you can start your work tomorrow. Have a good night." He waved and walked out the main classroom door.

"Really?" Artie said. "He thinks *that* was a great idea? I was *joking*. Are we sure he actually has an advanced degree and all?"

"Roll with it, dude," Paul said. "Just think how great it'll look on your college applications. You'll get into Harvard and Yale for sure."

"Either that or the only school who'll touch me with a ten-foot pole will be Miss Peregrine's Home for Peculiar Children. But wait, aren't you going to help me?"

"I don't know. You keep telling me how bad I am at it. I haven't been on Twitter or any social media since I screwed up that tweet to the jerky chess guy."

"I understand," Artie said. "You *are* pretty bad at it." He looked at his phone to see the time. "It's only three-fifteen. The after-school bus doesn't leave until four-thirty. If you need me,

I'll be in the library. I have to write another post card for my pen pal project."

Paul watched his friend jog out of the room. He turned back to find Sylvia staring at him. A half-smile crept across her face, showing the slightest hint of her dimples.

It was just the two of them.

Eight

Paul opened his mouth to speak but nothing came out. The empty room suddenly seemed too warm. There wasn't nearly as much air as there had been a few minutes earlier. The buses weren't leaving for over an hour. He wondered how long he could just stand there and stare awkwardly at Sylvia. Pretty long, probably.

Her dimples leapt into full bloom. "You doing anything right now?"

Paul's heart thumped in his chest. He hoped she couldn't hear it. "I dunno," he said.

She reached for his hand. "Come on."

She led him around the corridor and down two flights of stairs, to a corner of the building Paul didn't recognize, though he could smell chlorine so the pool must have been nearby. A few seconds later, she stopped in front of one of those two-part doors that had a top half and a bottom half. She motioned for Paul to knock.

He knocked. The upper door swung open. Paul saw a vast expanse of maroon and white, the school colors. He had to crane his neck to see the glowering faces of two gigunda football players, one African-American, wearing a game jersey with the number "86" on it, the other pale with a shaved head, wearing "69," which only made Paul giggle a little bit. Either of the behemoths, alone, would have been big enough to block the entire door. Together they made it impossible to see even a sliver of whatever was going on inside the room. They looked down at Paul and growled in unison.

"What do *you* want?" Number 86 said.

Sylvia poked her head over Paul's shoulder. "It's OK. He's with me."

Number 86's voice shifted into warmer registers. "Oh, Sylvia. Sorry, I didn't see you."

He opened the bottom half of the door. Paul gaped. Under the jerseys, the two football players wore matching black skirts with white polka dots, fishnet stockings, and humongous high heels, which made them both look at least 6'10".

86 clamped a shovel-sized hand on Paul's shoulder. His voice curdled again. "What are you looking at?"

Paul swallowed. "N-nothing. I was just imagining how hard it must have been to find pumps in that size."

"I know, right?" The big guy gave Paul a little slap on the shoulder. "And the stuff at the Big and Tall shop just isn't pretty." He stepped aside and gestured into the room. "Come on in."

The room was packed. Paul recognized a few faces but didn't know any names. Soon as they were out of earshot of the doormen, he asked Sylvia, "What is all this?"

"It's a meeting of the school's LGBTQ support group." She skipped on ahead, calling and waving to everyone.

Paul's stomach sank. What had he gotten himself into? He hurried to catch up with Sylvia, spoke quietly. "Are you... you know, any of those... letters?"

She turned to face him. "Are you asking me if I'm gay?"

Paul's face got hot. He put his hands on his cheeks. "Um, I guess. If it's not too personal?"

She laughed. "How much more personal can you get?" She gestured around the room. "These are my friends."

The chairs were arranged in a circle. Sylvia flopped into one and patted the seat next to her. Paul slumped down, eyes wide. To his knowledge, he'd never even spoken to a gay person before, though based on the familiar faces, he obviously had. Sylvia patted his cheek.

"The only rule is you can't talk about this to anybody outside this room. Everything shared must remain in confidence. You can't reveal any names to anyone. Not even to Artie."

Paul nodded. The others all sat down and the meeting began with everybody identifying themselves, though it all came too fast for Paul to remember anyone, except the football players, whose names were both John. Finally, he told them his own name.

Sylvia smiled at him. "Now they're your friends, too."

He felt dozens of eyes on him. Some wide with curiosity, others narrow with suspicion. The John with whom he'd discussed fashion gave him a little wink.

The group leader stood up. She spoke briefly about future events, including upcoming food drives for Thanksgiving and Christmas. Then she opened the discussion. People randomly stood and brought up a topic, and the others chimed in. They talked about being bullied, about facing harassment and prejudice. They talked about sports. Grades and college, confusion regarding their sexual identities, having a boyfriend or girlfriend for the first time, bridging the gap between being a child and an adult.

Paul didn't say anything, but he considered it. It surprised him that he already felt comfortable here, that so many of the topics resonated with him, had much more to do with being a baffled teenager than anything he might have called a "gay issue." Sylvia didn't speak, either, but every so often Paul felt her studying him. He bit his lip, afraid to meet her eyes.

The bell rang, announcing the impending departure of the after-school buses. The group dispersed. Sylvia walked next to Paul, humming to herself. When they reached the stairs, she leaned in close. She whispered in his ear.

"No, I'm none of those letters."

She got up on tiptoes and gave him a quick kiss on the cheek.

She circled in front to face him, nibbled her lip and gave a cute little toss of her short brown hair. Paul's stomach fluttered. He watched her wave and skip away toward her bus, his hand rubbing the spot her lips had touched.

Nine

Stanton headed to the Oval Office for the fourth time that day. The bright side was, according to his Fitbit, he was nearing his personal steps record. He entered the outer office area, where the President's personal secretary and personal aides sat just outside the Oval Office. Several figures milled about, sporting long white robes. Apparently Stew Cannon, alt-right darling and the President's "chief strategist," was somewhere around.

Stanton pushed past them. "Take those hoods off," he snapped. "This is the White House, for Christ's sake."

He knocked on the northeast door of the Oval Office, waited a respectful few seconds, then let himself in.

The President was behind his desk, talking on the phone. He was flanked on one side by Stew Cannon and on the other by Maryanne Monday, who had run the President's campaign and now served as "senior counselor."

"Absolutely, Danny. Buy all you can," the President said into the receiver.

Stanton hated to interrupt, but it was his job. "What are you buying, sir?"

An annoyed scowl crossed the President's face. He covered the receiver of the phone and glared at Stanton. "Me? I'm not buying anything. My children run the business now, remember? I'm just giving my middle son some valuable parental advice."

"I see." Stanton breathed in and held it, then released. "What is your son buying, sir?"

"Nothing to concern yourself about. War-ravaged real estate in southern Turkey."

He brought the phone back to his ear, but Stanton put out his hand. "I'm sorry, sir, but isn't the State Department about to wrap up a cease-fire agreement in southern Turkey?"

"The sellers don't know that. The important thing is this isn't a conflict of interest because I'm not personally involved in the transaction." He spoke into the phone again. "You understand, Danny. At the price I told you, and not a penny more. How long do you think it'll take? OK, got it."

He hung up the phone. "Before I forget, Stanton, tell the Secretary of State to dot every i and cross every t in that cease-fire agreement. Tell him to take a couple days if he has to. I don't want to announce anything until we're absolutely sure we got it perfect." He looked at Stew, he looked at Maryanne. "That should take at least a couple of days, right?"

They both nodded. President Passant addressed Stanton again. "Got that? A couple of days. Minimum. Also, I think we need to throw a press conference."

Stanton gave a solemn nod. "The Vice President resigning?"

"No, our Constitutional amendment. I understand it just passed the last statehouse?"

"That's right, sir. It's done," Stanton said. "Fastest passing of an amendment since the Bill of Rights."

Stanton swelled with pride. It may have been a stupid cause, but he and his staff had engineered an amendment to the *Constitution*. He'd never been part of such a historic accomplishment, of something that might last forever, much less been responsible for one. He attempted to make his expression humble, readied himself to bask in the President's recognition.

The President smiled. "You know, I have to hand it to me. That's what I call smart. Putting a little pressure on you petty bureaucrats is the only way to get things done in this town."

Stanton began humming his mantra under his breath, over and over.

"So let's hold a press conference to announce the Twenty-Eighth Amendment," the President said. "This Friday in Manhattan, lobby of Passant Place." The President leaned forward. "Are you humming?"

"Of course not, sir," Stanton said. "May I ask why New York?"

"Because it's a Friday and that's where I am on weekends. At least until the season starts in South Florida."

"Sir, the presidency is not a forty-hour-a-week job. I think it would look better if you briefed the press from the White House press room."

The President looked at Stew Cannon. He looked at Maryanne Monday. They both shook their heads. President Passant gritted his teeth.

"I am *not* spending my weekends in government housing. And that's final."

Stanton began humming under his breath again. "If you want to have the press conference this Friday, we'll have to find some reporters to attend," he said. "Last press conference, we only issued credentials to Brightbutt News and Fox. Correct me if I'm wrong, Stew, but isn't Friday the surprise party for Brightbutt's new editor? I can't imagine we want the optic of the President speaking to a lobby occupied only by Sam Hattery and his latest girlfriend?"

The President looked at Stew again. He looked at Maryanne. They both shrugged.

"Fine," he said. "Issue some press credentials. But *not* the failing New York Times or the Washington Post. Obviously not Buzzfeed, Politico, the Des Moines Register, or the Huffington Post, or any Spanish-language broadcasters. And *definitely* not CNN."

Stanton scribbled furiously in his notebook, made sure he got it all down. If nothing else, it might all be worth something when he wrote his memoir.

"Will that be all, sir?" he said.

The President looked at Stew and Maryanne. "What were we talking about before Stanton showed up?"

"Twitter won't divulge private subscriber information," Stew said. "No matter how nicely we ask. Or not nicely. Says it's their policy never to undermine the privacy rights and security of their users."

"Privacy rights? Did you tell them you work for the President of the United States?"

"I suspect telling them my name and title might have been the tipoff."

The President whipped out his phone. A moment later, Stanton's phone sounded the air raid siren. He noticed similar noises arising simultaneously from both Stew's and Maryanne's phones. Stanton looked at the display.

Edward N. Passant

@realEdwardNPassant

Twitter is for LOSERS!. Can't imagine anyone idiotic enough to use their outdated service.

3:27 PM - 26 Sep 2017

The President examined his handiwork. "All right, somebody has to help me delete that one." He handed his phone to Maryanne.

"Whose information are we asking them to divulge, sir?" Stanton said.

Without looking up from the President's phone, Maryanne slid her own phone across the President's desk. Stanton picked it up, read through a series of tweets, all of which showed the hashtag, #UpUrNPassant.

"It's trending number one," President Passant said. "You wouldn't believe some of the nasty things they're saying about me. Terrible. Not at all respectful of the President of the United States. I've tried hitting back, but I can't cut deep enough if I don't know anything about this 'Paul U-P,' who originated the hashtag. Can't even rankle him enough to provoke a response."

Stanton gave Maryanne her phone back. "Yes, it is terrible Mr. President, but that's what you get when your country allows free speech."

The President looked up. "Exactly!" His lips formed his trademark pout. "But that's a discussion for another day." He turned back to Stew. "So, let's hack them. How hard can that be? Don't tell me the *Russians* are better at it than the CIA? You have twenty-four hours before I get Vladimir on the phone."

"Excuse me, sir," Stanton said. "But it's illegal to use the CIA for domestic matters like this. Frankly, unless we have probable cause to believe this Paul U-P has committed a crime, I'm not sure we can use the FBI, either. Or any other intelligence agency."

The President snorted. He looked at Stew.

"I hate to admit it," Stew said. "But I think Stanton is right for once. We can't do this officially. It's got to be off the books." He rubbed the perpetual three-day stubble on his chin. "I play poker with the assistant director of the National Clandestine Service. He owes me a favor. Let me give him a call."

He chose an entry from his contact list, put the phone to his ear. He stepped to the side of the room and held a quiet conversation. Stanton couldn't hear what he was saying.

Instead, he faced the President. "Perhaps we ought to let this one go, sir. Perhaps a tweet war with a small-minded heckler isn't the best use of our resources."

"You know what, Stanton? You're right again. What does tweeting against him accomplish? The President frowned.

"We have to come up with something much worse."

Stew Cannon wore a grim smile when he returned. "It's taken care of. My buddy at NCS is more than happy to help. He says he has the *perfect* guy for us."

Ten

"That's all for now, Stanton," the President said. "Get this CIA agent over here then go do your job. I have a meeting."

He and his advisors trooped from the room. Stanton trailed out behind them. Fortunately, the Klan had vacated the outer office by the time Stanton got out there. He puttered around for a few minutes, looking at memos and such that had piled up on the personal secretary's desk. Occasionally, important missives slipped past Stanton's office and landed here, and the last thing Stanton wanted was President Passant to see and act on anything before it was vetted.

A colorful postcard caught his attention. "'Greetings from Area Fifty-One'?" he said to the secretary. "Have you been to Nevada recently?"

"Oh, no, Mr. Young," she said. "That card was addressed to the President."

"And you *gave* it to him?" He snatched the card off the desk and scrutinized the message on the back.

"I'm sorry, sir." At least she had the decency to look embarrassed. "He insisted. Said it's time to usher in that new era of American space leadership he promised during the campaign. He had me set up a meeting with NASA and an interpreter from SETI."

Stanton looked over the message again. "I don't think we need an extraterrestrial expert to translate Pig Latin, do we? It says, '*We're watching you. To acknowledge our communication, tug on your left ear the next time you broadcast a visual signal into space.*' Please tell me you can cancel the meeting."

"I'm afraid it's too late, sir. The NASA Administrator is already waiting in the Roosevelt Room. The President's heading over there right now."

Stanton trudged back to his office so he could go do his job.

*   *   *

Kayla Schwarzenegger — no relation to Arnold — walked rapidly through the Philadelphia Inquirer newsroom. Kayla did almost everything rapidly. In this case, she needed to rapidly find her editor and get permission to write a story that would appear somewhere other than the Style section.

She corralled him on his way to the men's room and blocked his path to the door.

She spoke rapidly. "You heard the Vice President just submitted his resignation? According to social media and other unnamed sources, while he was governor he had a man on payroll who roofied underage girls and brought them back to the statehouse for group sex."

Her editor eyed the rest room door. He tried to look like a man who wasn't crossing his legs. "What does the Vice President say about that?"

"He says it never happened."

"What does the White House say?"

"They say it's all over the internet." Kayla consulted her notes. "I had a few words with a senior aide in the V.P.'s office. The Veep insists he's being framed."

"A politician tries to get out from under a scandal? Big whoop. We get ten of those a week, it's not news anymore."

"Oh, well. It was worth a shot." Kayla flipped rapidly through her notepad. "How about nukes in North Korea? Terrorists on the French Riviera? Pennsylvania unemployment at record high?" She looked at his glazed eyes. "Martians landing in Kentucky?"

"We've been over this. It's not news until the President tweets it." He reached for the door handle. "So unless you have something that's not for the front section, will you please let me in there?"

Kayla flipped all the way to the last page of her notebook. She cringed. "There's an octopus at a local high school that posts its thoughts on Twitter."

The editor's hand slipped off the handle. "Intriguing. Tell me more."

"Not much more to tell. I checked and far as I can tell, it's not a prank. The school really has an octopus and the octopus really has a Twitter account."

"Now *that's* a story. I like it."

He twisted his torso around, folded his arms. He seemed to study Kayla for a moment. "But you'll have to put it off. I just got off the phone with the White House Chief of Staff's office. They're holding a press conference Friday in New York and this time they're actually letting press attend. I was going to give it to Rooney but he's too busy reporting on the UpUrNPassant hashtag. You might be just who we need."

He clasped her hand. "Congratulations, you're our new White House correspondent. You have three days to prepare. Good luck."

Without waiting for a response, he dodged around her and plunged into the men's room.

Kayla stared at the lavatory door for a long moment. She turned and walked rapidly back to her desk.

Eleven

If you didn't count the time his boss asked him to dress up like a clown and shoot a water pistol at a kids' birthday party, Seamus Callahan had only worked off the books once before. Not coincidentally, it had been his only previous mission on U.S. soil. The target had been some high up at a northern Virginia defense contractor, who'd been doing some off-the-books work himself, selling knock-off Stinger missiles to the Saudis. Even though his customer was an ally, selling the stuff without Congressional approval was generally considered to be a no-no in government circles. Seamus had researched the guy, shadowed him, and dispatched him in a back alley, to make it look like a common mugging.

Later, Seamus found out the guy had also been having an affair with the CIA director's married daughter.

It had bothered him. Not because of remorse. You couldn't shoot as many people as Seamus had and have a conscience, guilty or otherwise. No, what bothered Seamus was the feeling of being used. It had been the last mission he'd ever volunteered for.

Until now. This was different. This was the President of the United States, calling for Seamus to do his duty for his country. He'd been summoned to the Oval Office. Alone. It was obviously critical to national security.

Still, Seamus hadn't risen to the level of specialized skills officer by being incautious. His biggest fear, as he waited to be shown into President Passant's presence, was that he'd suffer another incident. He hoped the President didn't recognize him from the press conference fiasco, all those months ago.

His hand fiddled in his pocket as the White House secretary ushered him into the Oval. He looked around the room, visually examined the entire perimeter, peered into every shadow.

The President was alone, too.

Seamus came to attention.

"Agent Callahan? Have a seat." The President gestured to an armchair by the desk.

Seamus sat. He glanced around again, confirming nobody else was in the room. "What can I do for you, sir?"

"It's critical that I discover someone's true identity." The President slid a manila envelope across the desk. "All we know about him right now is his Twitter handle, but I'm sure you can find him, right?"

Seamus nodded. He wasn't the best hacker in the Agency, by a long shot, but a ten-year-old could hack an outfit like Twitter.

The President nodded back. "Excellent. Soon as you discover his identity and whereabouts, I want you to report directly to me. The phone number to call is in the packet." He sat back, stared at the ceiling for a few moments. When he continued talking, it seemed he was thinking out loud, not really speaking to Seamus at all.

"Nobody attacks me and gets away with it. And *nobody* ignores my tweets like that. I'm the President of the United States, godammit. I can do whatever I want to this guy. I can make him feel my power."

He blinked, looked up at Seamus. "I've got it. After you find him, we'll come up with a plan to draw him out. Just you and me. Then you'll make him disappear. Understand?"

Seamus stood up. "Of course, sir."

The President gave an approving nod. Seamus showed himself out. His hand fiddled in his pocket again.

He tapped the "record off" button on his phone.

*   *   *

The next morning, after first period, Paul was called down to the principal's office. He'd never been called to the principal's office before. He had no idea why he'd been summoned now.

Maybe they'd found out he and Artie had done lunch-and-learn in the Bio lab without permission? It hadn't even been Paul's idea, but he'd never rat out his best friend. But probably that wasn't it, since Artie wasn't with him now and, honestly, they'd only eaten a few of Orville's shrimp.

Could it have had something to do with the LGBTQ meeting? Incidents of hate and intolerance were up since President Passant had been elected, but Paul couldn't imagine the principal would be connected to anything like that. Besides, Paul wouldn't rat out those people, either. He hadn't even told Artie — well, he'd told him he went to the meeting, but not what they talked about and definitely not anyone who was in the room. He'd promised Sylvia he wouldn't.

But it had to be something. Paul gulped. What if he were expelled? He was good at math and science and social studies and stuff, he got good grades, but he didn't really have any marketable skills that might translate in a competitive workplace.

The principal came to the door of his office. He wore a suit and tie and leaned one hand on the doorframe, far above Paul's head. His mouth formed a straight line. "Mr. Urbina-Pedisich? Could you come in, please?"

Paul nodded. He flinched as he walked past the principal's upraised arm.

"Have a seat please, Mr. Urbina-Pedisich."

Paul did as he was told. The principal sat as well. He stared at Paul from across the desk.

"I heard something this morning," the principal said. "Something I frankly find a little difficult to believe. I thought we should discuss it."

This was it. Paul wondered if McDonald's accepted employment applications from short people with no marketable skills or a high school diploma. He knew Wal-Mart did, but probably only if he lived in Malaysia and was willing to work for 45 cents an hour.

"I received a phone call this morning," the principal said. "From the office of the President of the United States. Apparently, you've been awarded the President's Physical Fitness Award. The President wants to present it to you personally, this Friday in New York City."

"The President's Physical Fitness Award?" Paul said. "You sure they haven't confused me with someone who is, I don't know, physically fit?"

The principal nodded. "Your gym teacher was surprised, as well. But it doesn't seem to be a mistake. I've spoken with your parents and we all agree you should take an excused absence from school on Friday and accept the award in New York. It would be great publicity for the school and for the district. Plus I'm sure it will be a lot of fun. What do you say?"

"OK, I guess. It would probably be pretty cool to shake the President's hand and all."

That agreed, the principal sent Paul back to class. He practically ran down the halls. Sure, it probably would be boring, but Artie would go crazy when he heard. Paul stopped, bit his lip. How would Sylvia react? He didn't think she liked President Passant very much, but how many people get to meet the President of the United States, in person? Besides, everyone knew that only a total geek loser would turn down a free excused absence. He didn't want her to think *that* about him.

And anyway, it couldn't be too boring. Could it?

Twelve

Kayla had never been to a White House press conference before. Of course, in the past nine months, hardly anybody else had, either. She had three days to prepare. She stayed late each night, coming up with topics and questions and follow ups. By Friday morning, she thought she was ready.

The press conference had been called for 3pm. Kayla chose a train that got to New York two hours before that, just in case. She arrived at Passant Place and got through security an hour and a half early. The few reporters that had arrived were outnumbered by the techies setting up cameras and sound equipment. Kayla stood by one corner of the stage, drinking it all in.

"It's pretty exciting in person, isn't it?" a voice said from behind her.

Kayla turned to see who'd spoken. A man stood right behind her. He stuck out his hand. "Sam Hattery, Fox News."

"I know who you are." Kayla reciprocated the handshake. "You're practically the only person who can get an interview with President Passant. I'm Kayla Schwarzenegger, from the Philadelphia Inquirer."

"Schwarzenegger? Any relation to—"

"No," Kayla said. She had more than once considered finding a husband solely so she could change her last name. "But can I ask you something? I've heard the President frowns on certain questions. In this press conference, are there going to be limits on what we can ask him?"

"Absolutely not," a familiar voice boomed from behind her. Kayla began to tremble. The President himself stepped around the side of the stage. He seemed taller than he looked on TV.

He shook Sam Hattery's hand, then Kayla's. She introduced herself.

"Any relation to Arnold?" President Passant said.

Kayla put on her best smile. "No, sir. I've never even met him."

"I could arrange an introduction, if you'd like." He looked at Hattery. "Sam, your tech guy was looking for you. Sound check or some such. Seemed important."

Hattery smirked. "Yes, sir, Mr. President." He continued smirking over his shoulder as he walked away.

Kayla assumed the President would have to leave as well, get back to running the country or whatever, but he didn't move. Just stood there, smiling at her.

"So, you'll answer questions on any topic, today?" she said, mostly to divert the intensity of his stare.

"Sure, I'm as straight a shooter as they come," he said. "I'll answer absolutely anything, so long as it doesn't involve the Vice President, the Supreme Court, a potential conflict of interest, the latest jobs report, or anything about Russia, North Korea, China, Syria, Turkey, Iran, Iraq, Israel, or Mexico."

He looked around to make sure nobody was watching, then stepped right into Kayla's personal space. "So, think of a question. If it goes well, there might even be a one-on-one for you, later this evening. I'll have my head of security give you a special phone number to call." He popped a tic-tac into his mouth.

Blood rushed to Kayla's face. She couldn't find words to respond. She turned away, stumbled backward. She felt fingers brush across her left breast.

She swallowed the shout rising from her gut. It had to have been unintentional, she was the one who'd staggered, after all. He was the President of the United States. He'd never do such a thing in the middle of a crowded lobby. She began to calm down.

Then the President winked.

Kayla pretended to wave to an imaginary colleague. "Excuse me, sir." she said, before sprinting to her seat, as rapidly as her heels could take her.

She sat down and pressed her stomach to keep from throwing up.

Thirteen

Friday morning, 9:15. Seamus stopped by his favorite coffee shop on the way to Union Station. Not that he drank coffee anymore. Caffeine isn't good for narcoleptics. Makes it harder to regulate wakefulness. But he still frequented the shop, because it was the perfect place to upload large chunks of data. All you had to do was log in to the coffee shop's network, set the phone or other device to upload to an abandoned, virtualized sector of the Cloud, and just before closing time leave the device running behind a seat cushion in a secluded corner. Next morning, come early to the shop and "find" your lost device. If you did it right, nobody could trace the data to you, just to the coffee shop. Better, nobody seeking your secrets would have the slightest idea where to look.

He caught the 9:35 train to New York. He was dressed as a sound engineer, carrying a single piece of "equipment." He disembarked at Penn Station, NY, at 12:57pm. He caught a cab to Central Park, two blocks north of Passant Place.

He checked the time. Everything was on schedule. His phone beeped — a power warning, twenty percent. That sometimes happened with big uploads, but he couldn't deal with it now. Should still have plenty of juice left for his needs.

Security for the event was split among the Secret Service, the NYPD, and President Passant's private security force. Seamus went around to a pre-arranged door, guarded by a burly private security man with a thinning hairline and only nine fingers. After Seamus presented his press credentials and whispered a password, Nine Fingers let him through with a minimum of fuss.

He found a shadowed area next to a support column, near the sound equipment, with a clear view of the stage. He'd strapped a microphone to the end of his sniper rifle. Nobody who saw his silhouette would think "weapon." It threw the weight off, required an adjustment on his part, but that's why he'd practiced with it so much over the past three days.

He looked at his watch, left the rifle in its carrying case. Up close, it still looked like a gun. No need to take the chance of being spotted until the time was right. He had an hour and eight minutes until the press conference would begin. He turned on the Bluetooth receiver in his ear, chose the music he wanted, and leaned back in the dark to wait.

He began to relax, to regulate his breathing, slow his heart rate. This was essential for the well-trained sniper, but problematic for a narcoleptic. When he was relaxed, he was most susceptible to fall prey to an incident. That's what the music was for.

Not music he liked. That relaxed him even more. No, to stay awake, Seamus chose the most grating, most annoying music he could find, which at that moment was the collected works of Gordon Lightfoot. Listening to it made him want to bang his head against a wall, and those feelings made it somewhat more difficult to fall asleep. Eventually, he'd get used to the music, it would become familiar, and the problem would return. That was what had happened in Pyongyang.

Not this time. He wouldn't make that mistake twice. For this mission, he'd chosen something he hadn't heard in years, something he'd always hated.

3pm, the scheduled start time. Seamus made sure nobody was near enough to see more than his silhouette and began to set up. He took aim toward the approximate spot his target would occupy. Once the target came on the stage, he'd readjust. He hoped the press conference would start on time.

It didn't. Nobody came onto the stage. The reporters, technical people, and political staff all still milled about the lobby. They made no move to find their seats. Gordon Lightfoot's voice assaulted Seamus in stereo.

Sometiiiiiiimes, I think it's a sin, when I feel like I'm winning, when I'm losing again…

A half-hour passed, more. Finally, somebody came on stage. Not the President, someone giving an introduction, a rather lengthy one. President Passant didn't get to the podium until after 4:15pm. Seamus's breathing and heart rate were exactly where he wanted them. He hoped they'd call the target to the stage sooner, rather than later.

Again, they didn't. The President started with a soliloquy, didn't even ask for questions yet. He seemed to be talking to himself again. He went on and on and on.

No matter. Seamus was used to waiting. He stared down the barrel of his rifle. Motionless.

His phone beeped again.

Seamus ignored it.

Fourteen

The President went on and on and on. Kayla hardly heard him. She sat alone in the crowded room.

She felt a powerful urge to tell these strangers what had happened, to stand on her chair and shout it out to the world, but an even more powerful urge not to. Ever. To clamp her mouth shut. If she didn't speak of it, she wouldn't have to think about it. The two urges fought in her mind. Her head throbbed. She paid little attention to the room around her.

A distraction might tip the balance. Something to occupy her thoughts long enough to convince herself her encounter with President Passant had never happened. Maybe if she set her mind to her job, it could all work out.

"What's with the President?" a female voice said from the seat next to her. "He keeps pulling on his left ear."

Kayla looked up. The woman was in her mid-sixties. She had a familiar face. Kayla had seen her on television many, many times. She'd always considered the woman kind of a hero. Despite herself, she felt a small thrill, felt herself take a baby step closer to functional.

Maybe she could tell this woman what had happened? No, that would be stepping in the wrong direction. Instead, she said, "Seems like we're at one of his rallies, with him riffing on whatever pops into his head. I zoned out for a moment, has he done his aria on the dishonest, fake news media?"

"Twice now." The woman stuck out her hand. "I'm Andrea Robinson, from—"

"I know who you are. My name is Kayla Schwarzenegger."

"That's a burden," Andrea said. "This your first presidential press conference, Kayla?"

Kayla nodded. "I know you've been to zillions."

"This is my ninth president." Andrea nodded. "Although none of the others went with a Briefing Gone Wild theme." She pointed to the back of the room, where a dozen or so buxom young women with impossibly small waists bounced and cheered the President's every word. "I mean, seriously, rented Playboy bunnies on the rope line? A spin room operating full bore, right there next to the stage, translating from the opening minute?" She shook her head.

"Translating into other languages?"

"No, it's Maryanne Monday and her staff, telling whoever'll listen what the President really means."

Kayla glanced at the bunting and colored lights, the giant screen behind the stage, depicting the President way larger than life. She refused to look at his smirking, overly magnified mouth.

"First press conference I've been invited to since Passant won the election, though," Andrea said. "He's really upped the ante since the campaign. Guess it's easier to go whole hog when you're funded by the people's tax dollars and not out of your own pocket."

President Passant had started talking about the new Constitutional Amendment. To hear him tell it, he'd conceived, researched, drafted, and personally calligraphed the thing, all by his lonesome. He began to wax poetic about the future of the nation's most important piece of paper, pointing out that 1789 was a long time ago and nothing could get that old without requiring some sort of overhaul. He had some additional ideas for constitutional changes. The First Amendment, in particular, was in dire need of modernization. He went on and on and on.

"Does the Constitution even have an Article Eight?" Kayla said after a particularly puzzling presidential pronouncement.

Andrea laughed. "Not yet."

"You think he'll get to questions and answers soon?"

"Twenty or thirty minutes. But don't worry, he won't call on either of us. It'll be all pre-arranged softballs from Fox and other members of the conservative press."

Kayla laughed, perhaps a little too maniacally. "I bet I could make him call on me."

"Yeah, how?"

"Take off my shirt."

Andrea gave her a grandmotherly hug on the shoulder. "Not worth it, honey. He might call on you but he still wouldn't answer your question." She stood up. "Come on, let's go see if Maryanne Monday thinks the President really wants to reinstitute slavery."

Kayla could almost smile. Yeah, this was what she needed. Her encounter with the President was beginning to fade away, become foggy, like the remnants of an unpleasant dream.

They walked to the side of the lobby, slipped behind the camera operators and sound engineers to make their way to the side of the stage. The President opened things up for questions. As Andrea predicted, the first person he called on essentially asked him to repeat what he'd been saying for the last fifteen minutes.

"The Founding Fathers didn't know much, OK?" the President said. "They didn't know anything. I mean, these are the guys who brought us the French and Indian War. I know much more than the Founding Fathers, believe me. They wrote a broken document, and I'm the only one who can fix it."

The two reporters kept walking. They reached a shadowed area, not far from the stage. They stopped to listen to the next question, about some obvious gaffe the Attorney General had made that morning. The President responded by talking some more about the Constitution. Then he said, "Before I take any more questions, I have someone I'd like to introduce to you all."

Kayla looked at Andrea, who shrugged and shook her head. The President waved to someone standing in the far wing. A boy, early teens, took a hesitant step onto the stage, then another, coaxed on by President Passant.

Kayla could tell the boy's mother had picked out his clothes and combed his hair for him. She couldn't tell why he'd been invited onto the stage. The reporters in the seats, similarly baffled, began talking and whispering amongst themselves.

A premonition shivered Kayla's spine. She couldn't pinpoint why. The buzz of the crowd rose, to the point where she couldn't hear much of anything. Andrea said something but Kayla couldn't make it out. The President spoke but even at the tremendous volume emitted by the gigantic speakers, it sounded to Kayla like the adults in a Charlie Brown cartoon. Maybe something about physical fitness? The juxtaposition of the bright lights on the stage and the dark shadows around her confused her sight, made it impossible to focus on anything nearby.

The boy seemed stiffer than the life-sized cardboard cutouts of President Passant that were scattered throughout the room. The kid's eyes reflected the hot stage lights, he probably couldn't see a thing. His whole body trembled as he reached up to return the President's handclasp.

Directly in front of Kayla, somebody screamed.

Not a bouncy scream of adoration from the Playboy bunnies. This was a scream of terror or anguish. The crowd gasped. The President and the boy froze, hands an inch or two from each other. Kayla froze too. She couldn't move a muscle.

The scream rose again.

President Passant looked directly into the shadows surrounding Kayla. On the big screen, calculations ran across his eyes.

With both hands, he pushed the boy out in front of him.

The President stumbled backward. His hands rose to shield his face. He dove flat to the floor and rolled toward the far side. Secret Service agents and private security guards raced up to pull him off the stage.

The boy stood at the front of the stage, flatfooted. Shoulders hunched, mouth hanging open, eyes wide, like a deer caught in a hunter's sights.

The scream rang out for the third time. This time Kayla could make out what it said.

"GUUUUNNNNNNNN!!!!!!!"

The crowd scattered. Maryanne Monday's spin area dispersed. Middle-aged reporters trampled Playboy bunnies on their way to safety. Desperate camera and sound people knocked over their own equipment. Their exodus opened a sightline for Kayla.

She saw the gun. And the gunman. He'd propped himself against a support column, shoulders relaxed, weapon steady, pointed toward the hapless child on the stage. The President, presumably the assassin's target, was long gone. The shooter didn't waver.

The boy was alone. He was about to die.

Kayla's stasis shattered. She had a clear path to the gunman, didn't know if she could get there on time. She sprinted forward, faster than she'd ever moved in her life. She gathered herself to spring, punch, kick, anything that might jar the gunman's aim. Her mouth formed a defiant shout.

She stopped, breathing hard, a few steps from the assassin. The urgency drained out of her. The man wasn't going to shoot.

He was snoring.

Fifteen

They tossed him into solitary confinement. Didn't bother Seamus much. He'd been in prisons before, and in much nastier places like Turkey, and Kansas.

The way he knew he wasn't in Turkey or Kansas now was the amount of time that passed between the moment the Secret Service roughly jostled him awake and trussed him up and the moment they dumped him here. He was somewhere in the New York metropolitan area. Which would work out fine.

He wasn't sure how long he'd been locked in the cell. He'd fallen asleep twice now for who knew how long. Jail cells didn't bother him, but they were fairly boring. He felt himself drifting off again when he heard a familiar voice, coming from the slot in the door.

"You're in major shit, Seamus."

Seamus shook himself out of his lethargy. He knew that voice. They'd served together for years, been friends ever since Seamus had rescued his future boss from a brothel in Fallujah where, unbeknownst to the American agents, the ladies' definition of "giving head" involved handing their client's severed extremity to the nearest ISIS recruiting station.

"You think?" Seamus said. "Thanks, I hadn't noticed."

His boss said something to the guards. Their steps trailed further down the hall. Seamus moved close to the door, stooped to the slot. He kept his voice low. "They're painting it like I was attempting to assassinate the President?"

"What'd you expect? Flowers?"

Seamus shrugged. What did bother him was people thinking he betrayed his country. Like that time with the CIA director's daughter, he felt like a dirty washrag.

'Doesn't matter, anyway," his boss said. "Think the reaction would be better or worse if they knew you were planning to kill an innocent child in cold blood?"

"*You* sent me to him. This was *his* plan. I was only following orders."

His boss's voice became muffled, like he'd turned his head to the side. "You don't get it, do you, Seamus? The public is upset because you tried to kill someone. The people who count are pissed because you fell asleep again."

"My phone ran out of juice. The President spoke longer than he was supposed to."

"Who cares? You're done, Seamus. Nobody's going to rescue you this time. Especially not the President. You never met. He's never heard of you. Official story is you went rogue, decided to shoot President Passant after you got fired in disgrace."

"But I haven't been fired."

His boss didn't bother to respond. Seamus had been cast adrift. Not surprising, just a bit disappointing. He wasn't crazy about his backup plan, he had professional ethics to uphold, after all. But he was a lot less enamored with the alternative.

His boss said, "You'll be tried in a military tribunal on a base in the Philippines. Or at least that's the official word. In real life, they won't actually bother with the trial. The lethal injection's all ready."

His voice lowered to a whisper. "I truly am sorry, Seamus. Before the narcolepsy, you really were one of our best. And a loyal friend, too. You deserve better."

"Whatever," Seamus said. "Can you at least do me one favor before you ship me off to Manila? You owe me that much. For Fallujah, if not the rest of it."

Seamus took the silence as a yes. "Thanks," he said. "Tell the Democratic National Committee I have something they should find valuable. Tell 'em to bring their computer guys. And their lawyers."

Seamus inhaled the putrid prison air. He never thought it would come to this. Then again, he never thought he'd have Gordon Lightfoot on his iPhone, either. Life was funny that way.

He wasn't ready for his to end.

"It's time for me to play Let's Make a Deal," he said.

His boss didn't respond. Seamus wasn't sure when he left. Next thing he knew, he was lying on the hard cement floor, waking up with a splitting headache.

Sixteen

"There's a copy of it *where?*" President Passant slapped his hand on the Resolute desk, near where he'd carved his initials, directly above JFK's.

"A virtualized sector of the — do you care, sir?" Stanton said. "The key phrase is, 'There's a copy.' A recording of the discussion between you and your trained killer, to which the assassin has kindly given access to the DNC, which is currently negotiating with CNN and MSNBC to see who gets to break the news first."

"I don't get it," the President said. "For a guy who shoots people for a living, he seemed fairly savvy. Why give your leverage away like that? Why not come to us?"

Stanton wondered if he'd meditated sufficiently that morning. "*Because* he is fairly savvy, Mr. President. He knew he'd fall prey to an unfortunate 'accident' fifteen minutes after he told us. He got a message through to my office an hour ago. Says if we let him vanish off the grid on his own terms, he'll make sure he's not available to testify, and all they'll have is an unauthorized wiretap, which is not permissible evidence in court. Pretty clever, actually."

The President got up and fixed himself a Scotch. "It's hard to fathom, Stanton. Almost destroys my faith in humanity. Whatever happened to putting country first? I'm his commander in chief, how could he throw me under the bus like that?"

"To be fair, Mr. President, it was only after you shoved him into the fender that he tried to drag you under with him."

"Since when have I ever cared about being fair?" The President shook his head, as if unable to imagine a world where he couldn't count on absolute loyalty from people he'd discard at a moment's notice. "You really think we ought to give him a get out of jail free card?"

"We can't try him in a military tribunal now. Public outcry and all that. And if we disappear him, everybody'll know it was us. We'd get crucified in the press. Worst of all would be a domestic trial, if he was around to give evidence. You'd be in it as well, sir, and deep. Even Presidents aren't allowed to conspire to murder innocent civilians."

The President made a face, like he was about to ask for another constitutional amendment. Instead, he said, "Play the tape again."

Stanton pressed the button and they listened to the recording for the seventeenth time. As the critical quote sounded, the President slammed his fist into the wall.

After you find him, we'll come up with a plan to draw him out. Just you and me. Then you'll make him disappear. Understand?

"This is much ado about bullshit," President Passant said. "'Make him disappear' could mean anything. Tell me, why would I need to kill the kid when we could hold him indefinitely at Gitmo or someplace? Probably without even any waterboarding. After what he said about me on Twitter? Come on, he deserved it."

Stanton whipped around to make sure the door was shut tight. "Please don't ever say that out loud again, Mr. President." He wiped his brow. "Although small favors, at least you had sense enough not to tweet it."

The President shuffled his feet. On cue, Stanton's phone went off like an air raid siren.

Stanton hummed his mantra, but it wasn't helping. "I also heard from the Minority Leader about your real estate deal in Turkey. Did you really think the press wouldn't figure it out?"

"Wasn't me, it was my son Danny. I'm not officially connected to the company, anymore, remember?"

"Either way, it couldn't have come at a worse time, Mr. President. The Dems are firing up the bar-b-q as we speak. We're going to be slathered in sauce by nightfall."

"Let 'em try," President Passant said. "I didn't break any laws. I checked with the Counsel's office. There's no law against the President having a conflict of interest."

"That's technically correct, Mr. President." Stanton eyed the President's wet bar, wondering whether hard liquor and hallucinogens would work better than yoga. "They can't convict you of a conflict of interest. But there's definitely a law against the President abusing his authority."

"Really?" President Passant sat back down at his desk. "What law is that?"

Stanton looked at the bar again. He looked at the President.

"What law did you think, sir? A little thing called *impeachment*."

Seventeen

Every channel had it by 6pm. The President's voice on the incriminating tape while the screen showed a close-up of his sly expression as he shoved the boy out front of him, toward the gunman only President Passant knew about. The same video on all the broadcast networks, plus CNN, MSNBC, and a host of others on cable. All but Fox, which ran b-roll of Maryann Monday insisting that when the President said, "make him disappear," he was talking about hiring a magician for his son Prince's upcoming ninth birthday party. Sam Hattery did an in-depth interview with the soon-to-be nine-year-old about his fascination with David Copperfield.

The President refused to look at the television. He chose instead to watch gifs of the same clip on Twitter, in post after post employing the hashtag #UpUrNPassant. His face got redder and redder. He found a longer clip on Brightbutt News, showing the events on stage after he shoved the boy, and his voice perked up.

"That's an impressive barrel-roll on my part, don't you think, Stanton? Bet you can't name another president who could make that move under pressure like that. And that dive? I could do all my all own stunts."

Stanton turned off the TV. "You may get your chance sooner than you'd planned, sir."

"Lighten up, Stanton. I survived the Russia witch hunt and came through the FBI obstruction thing without a scratch. You really think they'd impeach me over *this*?"

"With every news organization reporting you put out a hit on an innocent fourteen-year-old child and used classified information to buy underpriced real estate for your next hotel? I'm going to go with yes."

"See, there it is, more fake news!" The President pointed at the television as if he wanted it incarcerated. "The kid was *fifteen*, not fourteen. The press is just lying, not a shred of decency." His lower lip protruded with indignation. "How come nobody holds *them* accountable?"

He picked up his phone and started typing.

"Please don't tweet that, Mr. President," Stanton said. "If just twenty-two Republicans cross the aisle, they'll impeach you in the House. Then they'll need only nineteen R's to convict you in the Senate. It's going to happen. No amount of spin can fix it."

The President went back to surfing Twitter. "Then what?" he said.

"Since the Vice President resigned last week, the Speaker of the House would take over as President. Used to be, in situations where there was no President or Vice President, Congress would have the option of calling a special presidential election, but since they changed the Presidential Succession Act in 1947, it's not clear whether they still can, especially after the Twenty-Fifth Amendment clarified that section of the Constitution."

"And if I resign, the same thing?"

Stanton nodded. The President grabbed the receiver for his hot line. "Get me Stew Cannon." He set the receiver down and looked up at Stanton. "If we offered the Minority Leader my resignation in exchange for changing the law back the way it was, you think she'd bite?"

"She'd jump at it, given the choice between a fair shot in a special election versus a certain three years of either you or the Speaker in the big chair. Between the Dems and our friends who don't like Speaker O'Brien very much, it would have a good chance of passing."

"When would the special election take place?"

"In the old law, early- to mid-December, eight or ten weeks from now."

"And how would the nominating process go?"

"I'd have to check the RNC bylaws, but ten weeks isn't enough time to hold primaries. Probably a simple vote of the national committee. Where are you going with this, sir?"

The President polished off his third Scotch. "It's simple, Stanton. If I resign, they can't impeach me. We'll campaign for a couple months, win again, and be right back in the driver's seat, like none of this ever happened."

Stanton wondered whether, if he started mainlining heroin, this would all just seem funny. "I'm not sure it's that easy, sir. Certainly, Senator Diaz would have something to say about—"

"Lyin' Ned? Who I already beat?" The President spoke loudly to drown Stanton out.

"And Senator Hernandez has gained a lot of—"

"Beat him."

"Not to mention, Governor Kramer—"

"Trounced him."

"Jedd Shrubb might want another—"

"Kicked his girlie ass all the way down Main Street."

Stanton sucked in a huge breath and spoke as fast as he could, to avoid further interruptions. "The guy we'd most have to watch out for is Vice President Panze."

"Panze? After he resigned in disgrace?"

Stanton blinked. "Really, sir?"

Stew Cannon let himself into the Oval. President Passant waved away Stanton's concern. "Don't worry about Manchester. Stew will take care of him — won't you, Stew? In fact, let's arrange it so Panze and I are the top two vote-getters, then we'll drop the bomb just before the runoff. He won't stand a chance. That leaves us eight or so weeks to campaign against the Democrats. They'll nominate Alison Denton again, right? The nasty woman I beat in a landslide less than a year ago?"

Stanton said nothing for a few moments, debating whether the term "landslide" could appropriately be used to describe an election in which the winner got three million fewer votes than his opponent. He shrugged.

"Probably," he said. "Who else could they nominate?"

Eighteen

Kayla cruised up the Schuylkill Expressway in suburban Philadelphia. It had been a few days since the press conference and she was starting to feel a little better. She could almost believe her "brush" with the President had been a figment, and she could just go about her job, same as she always did. Her phone rang and she activated her car's Bluetooth interface.

"Kayla, where are you?" her editor's voice came through the car's speakers.

She looked at her GPS. "On my way to Ardmore, to interview the tweeting octopus."

"Thought I said you didn't have to do that?"

He'd said a lot of things in the aftermath of the assassination attempt. Kayla's new friend Andrea Robinson had done a live segment on national television. She'd interviewed Kayla, made her out to be a hero, the woman who ran *toward* the gunman when everyone else ran away. After that, all the other news outlets wanted interviews, as well. Kayla traded a few minutes of her time for access and future favors. She was now the most connected junior reporter on the Eastern seaboard. She could have her editor's job in a minute, if she wanted it, and he knew it too.

She exited the highway and turned left at the bottom of the ramp. "You did," she said. "Except guess who helps take care of the octopus?"

"If it's not one of the Kardashians—"

"Close," Kayla said. "Paul Urbina-Pedisich."

"Who? Wait, the kid from the press conference?"

"Bingo. He apparently also originated the UpUrNPassant hashtag. Between that and surviving a presidential hit team, he might be the most popular person in America right now."

"Whoa, that *is* news. You should definitely reschedule it."

"I beg your pardon?"

"I assume you heard the President's announcing his resignation at noon tomorrow," her editor said. "I've wrangled you a sit-down with Lincoln Echols Creed, tonight."

"The veteran Democratic political operative?"

"You got it. There's going to be a special election, and Creed's heading the selection subcommittee for the Dems. I need you in Washington by seven p.m."

Kayla checked the time. She slammed the brakes, skid into a U-turn, and gunned back onto the highway. The octopus would have to wait.

Three and a half hours later, she pulled into a street spot not far from a dive bar on the outskirts of Georgetown.

Lincoln Echols Creed was a skinny African-American man who was about 60 but appeared at least 15 years older, with a face and hairless head so shriveled he resembled a walking raisin. He waited for her at a rickety table in the far corner of the dingy saloon, nursing a beer while he watched her approach.

His attire was at odds with the surroundings, a suit worth more than the bar's entire furniture budget and shoes shinier than any Kayla had seen since her friend Mary Ellen got sprung from Catholic school.

He spoke in a deep, tobacco-stained voice. "I know you. You're that hero-woman. Saw you on the teevee." He motioned for her to take the wobbly chair opposite him at the table.

Kayla reached out her hand while her words tumbled over each other. "Kayla Schwarzenegger, thanks for the interview. It's certainly a historic time for our country."

He didn't ask if she was related to Arnold, just rocked in his chair as if he didn't care about trivial details like that. But one look into his squinting brown eyes told her that he already knew she wasn't. That he knew a lot of things.

She set her phone on the table, brought up the recording app and got it running. "Shall we get down to it?"

He rocked back and forward, forward and back. "We could use a hero round here," he said. "That's the problem with this town, not enough heroes."

Kayla chewed her tongue, not at all sure what to make of the man. "Can we start with some background?" she said. "How did the party go about selecting the subcommittee that will choose the next Democratic nominee?"

He polished off his drink, signaled to the lone server in the joint for another. "Our subcommittee doesn't choose anything," he said. "We just make recommendations. Full Democratic National Committee chooses the nominee by majority vote, the way they do in civilized nations."

"I see," Kayla said. "And how much weight does your 'recommendation' carry with the full DNC?"

The faintest hint of a smile played across his face. "Fair amount."

Kayla wasn't about to let his folksy act divert her from her story. She pushed ahead. "I assume it's going to Alison Denton again — third time's a charm?"

Creed kept rocking. He smiled at the server when she brought his beverage, offered her a piece of unsolicited career-advancement advice. He turned back to Kayla. "Doubt it."

"Going with Burton Flanders this time?"

He sipped his beer, gave a soft harrumph. "That train left the station some time ago."

"Excuse me? Who else is there? Denton and Flanders were the only people who ran in the primaries. There hasn't been time for anybody else to get sufficient name recognition."

He took another swig. "Mmm, that's damn good. You ever have a nice Märzen, early October, when it's fresh?"

She swallowed her impatience. "I'm not really a beer person."

"That so?" He cocked his head to one side, as if considering the best way to tell her about a stain on her blouse. Kayla gripped her hands together, watched her fingertips go white with the strain of waiting quietly.

"Can I let you in on a secret, hero-woman?" he said at last. "Why don't you turn off your recorder and just listen for a bit?"

Kayla did as she was asked. She stared at Lincoln Echols Creed and held her breath.

He took another sip of beer. He leaned forward.

"We in the political arena have to face facts," he said. "Hard for an old-timer like me to admit it, but it's not like it was. The equation's been changing for a long time, but the last election proved it beyond doubt."

"The fractured demographics of our country?"

"Well, no. And yes, I suppose. It's the anger. Everybody's so angry. They always were, of course, but now it's different, somehow. How they take out their rage has changed. Manifests itself in many ways, but especially in the big offices. Meaning, if you're running for top dog, you don't need experience, or talent. No need to be scandal-free anymore, don't have to tell the truth. You don't even need to come off as a decent human being. You just need one thing."

Kayla's voice lowered on its own, down almost to a whisper. "And what's that?"

Creed let out a soft chuckle. "You just need to be something *different*. Something they've never seen before. Anything but the same old, same old." He shook his head. "And apparently not a woman. No offense."

Kayla nodded. That was certainly what had happened in the last presidential election. And sort of in the election eight years before that. The idea of the first black President had energized a lot of people in 2008. The idea of the exact opposite had brought millions out of the woodwork in 2016. But what was left? What sort of person could carry the shock value Lincoln Creed was looking for?

"So, you're thinking Latino?" she said. "Asian? You don't think a gay person could win a national election, do you?"

Creed stood up, his pricey suit hanging loosely on his sparse frame. He threw some money on the table.

"You drove down here?"

She nodded.

"Then we can discuss it on our way back up to Philly."

"What? Who's in Philadelphia?" She mentally ran through the list of Philadelphia-area elected officials who might fit the bill. Nobody stuck out.

Creed chuckled again. Kayla's eyes widened. "No! You don't mean the kid, Urbina-Pedisich? He's years away from being old enough to vote, much less run for office."

"That sort of thing hasn't mattered in *weeks*," Creed said. "We got ourselves a new Constitutional Amendment, remember?"

"But why would you even want to run a high school sophomore for President of the United States?"

"You kiddin'?" Creed slipped into his expensive overcoat. "He's the most popular person in America."

Nineteen

Heath Dunbar crouched down to scrub the underside of the toilet. He often got stuck with latrine duty during his Friday to Sunday retreats with the Lycoming County Pennsylvania Volunteer Militia. It wasn't easy stretching his 6'6" 275-pound frame into those hard-to-reach areas between the stalls, but he didn't mind so much since he'd purchased the rubber gloves and nose plugs.

He'd joined the private volunteer militia on his 21st birthday. His father was in the LCPVM. His grandfather had been in the LCPVM. Perhaps more importantly, at least to Heath, his fiancé's father and grandfather were in the LCPVM, as well. She'd only been his girlfriend when he'd joined up, but the look on her face at his induction ceremony had promised more. Three generations, on both sides. Heath wondered why they couldn't have come up with a more aesthetically pleasing acronym.

The organization had been around for more than fifty years, organized as a response to the hippy-dippy craziness of the '60s for the express purposes of defending individual rights and property against a tyrannical government, for paramilitary training and emergency response, and for commandeering the TV at the Stars-and-Stripes Tavern, next to LCPVM headquarters in Williamsport, PA. The town of 30,000 had been natural soil for a group like this, as the only thing the good people of Williamsport held more dear than their right to bear arms was their right to host the Little League World Series.

Heath believed in the 2nd Amendment, too, though after carefully studying the wording of the Amendment and the legislative history from 1787, he wasn't exactly sure how a law explicitly applicable to "a well-regulated militia" gave individuals an absolute right to fire 900 rounds a minute.

Then again, Heath wasn't sure about a lot of things. He was not considered the sharpest piece of cheddar on the cheese board by his peers. In fact, most everybody he knew considered him a bit slow, dating back to his childhood when he had towered over all the other kids. People took one look at him and assumed he was much older than he was, had expected him as a four-year-old to display the intellectual and emotional depth of his eight- and nine-year-old neighbors.

Eventually, he had conformed to become what everyone already thought of him — slow. His movements were deliberate; he didn't speak much but when he did he employed an unhurried drawl. He worked with meticulous care, but people tended to notice how much time he spent rather than how few mistakes he made. Took him forever to finish reading a book while he strove to examine and fathom every single word, but read he did, constantly and on many subjects. He was endlessly curious, about mysteries such as how come the plural of "sheep" is "sheep," and why non-comedogenic skin moisturizer just isn't funny.

A fellow private came to fetch him. "Colonel wants to see everybody at the mustering spot," he said, referring to the booth at the Stars-and-Stripes closest to the television.

Heath rose slowly and followed his fellow out of headquarters and next door to the tavern. He saluted the Colonel.

"If the rumors are true, it's a sad day for America," the Colonel said. "President's about to give his speech, after they get done with Apes on Tape." He pointed at the television, where a skinny African-American man with a face and bald head like a raisin was talking to an attractive, female Fox News reporter.

"Why do you call it that?" Heath said.

"Look at him," the Colonel said. "From Africa, obviously, like his orangutan ancestors. We'd all be better off if they'd stayed there."

Heath scratched his head. "You come from a German heritage, don't you, sir?"

"Bet your ass," the Colonel said. "One hundred percent pure."

"Well, sir," Heath drew out his carefully worded reply. "The Lusitanian slug is a common pest endemic to the forests of southern Germany, near the homes of your ancestors. Does that make you a spineless sl—"

"Latrine duty, Private!" The Colonel thrust his index finger toward the exit. "Right now!"

Twenty

Now that Paul had nearly been shot and killed, not to mention interviewed by more or less every channel on basic cable, he was a big celebrity at school. The principal had given him most of the week off, so he could "deal with his psychological distress," but Paul had a quiz he didn't want to miss on Friday so he got over his trauma and caught the bus that morning.

The jocks had insisted he take their seats during lunch-and-learn. And getting through the halls was almost as big an ordeal as anything else he'd been through, with everybody grabbing at his hand or patting his back, even the teachers. Took him twenty minutes to get from his locker to Mr. Harrison's classroom after school.

He'd barely gotten through the Bio lab door when a very short, very skinny missile launched herself at him and threw her arms around his neck.

"Ohmigod, ohmigod, I was so worried," Sylvia said. Paul kind of liked the way her body pressed close to his, so he didn't say much of anything until she let go of him and stepped back.

"Are you OK?" she said.

"I'm fine. The guy didn't actually shoot me or anything. He got bored and dozed off." He looked around the lab. "How's our favorite octopus?"

Artie sat near the tank, doing something with a bucket and a small knife. "He's great. We taught him how to say 'yes' and 'no,' using a waterproofed switch and a couple of lights." He pointed at a confusing jumble of electrical wires on the far side of the tank.

Paul peered at his friend, who continued whatever he was doing with the bucket. "What do you got going on there?" Paul said.

"I'm peeling the shrimp for Orville."

"You know, in the wild, he eats them live. I don't think he needs utensils and a napkin."

"Shows what you know. You ever eat one of those shrimp tails by mistake? Yuck! And it's not like Orville has teeth or anything. Just that funny little beak down in his butt."

"I'm pretty sure that's not his butt," Sylvia said. "I mean, with his mouth there, it can't be, right?"

Artie went right on shucking shrimp. "I heard your little bro had some trauma of his own," he said to Paul. "Did you really turn his skin all blue?"

"Biochemistry at its finest. That's what comes from paying attention in class." Paul held up both fists in a strong-man pose. "I have the knowledge and I'm not afraid to use it."

Sylvia covered her mouth with one hand. "Wait, what did you do to him?"

"Nothing, he's fine. Just a little Smurf-like for a couple days, that's all."

"Your own brother?" She backed away a couple steps.

Artie came to Paul's rescue. "Frankly, he's more demon-spawn than sibling. You wouldn't believe the grief Paul gets from the little creature. Kid makes the Joker and the Riddler look like social workers."

There was a knock at the door. All three kids gaped for a moment. Mr. Harrison opened it and walked in, followed by both of Paul's parents and the hot-looking reporter who'd tried to save Paul's life in New York, plus an old African-American man with a very wrinkled face.

"Paul, these people are here to see you," Mr. Harrison said.

Paul instinctively looked to his mother, but she turned her glance toward the old man. He stepped forward and shook Paul's hand.

"Hello, Paul. My name is Lincoln Creed, and I work for the Democratic National Committee." His tone was different from most adults when they spoke to Paul and his friends, not dismissive or condescending at all. Paul straightened his typical teenage slouch and looked straight at the man.

"I assume you know the President of the United States resigned today?" Mr. Creed said.

Paul nodded. "We watched it in American History class."

"Excellent. You probably also heard there's a special election in a couple months. I've spent most of the day talking to your parents about this, and we all agreed it was time to come talk to you." The man smiled. "Paul, how'd you like to run for President of the United States?"

Nobody spoke for what seemed like hours, like they didn't want to admit they hadn't heard right. Paul blinked. President of the United States? While he hadn't gotten expelled the previous week, this was still way better that McDonalds. Or Wal-Mart.

"Am I allowed to do that?" he said.

"You sure are," Mr. Creed said. "The question is whether you *want* to do it."

Artie was hopping up and down. "You should totally do it, dude. I mean, if you're President, you can give *yourself* a physical fitness award. How cool would that be?"

"What would I have to do?" Paul said to Mr. Creed.

"Good question," Paul's Dad said.

"Indeed," Mr. Creed said. "First, you'd have to do a fair number of interviews, but I watched you on the teevee over the weekend and I thought you did great. You'd have to give a few speeches, which I'll help you with. You'll give them at rallies — we'll stick to Eastern and Midwestern swing states and keep overnight travel to a minimum. Maybe a few grip-and-grins, though the DNC will be taking care of the fundraising. Plus one debate. We'll get the date from the commission, but I'm guessing the night of Tuesday November 14, and you'll have to prep for a few days before that.

"Hold on," Paul said. "I can't go to a debate on November 14. I have the PSAT the next morning."

"Well," Mr. Creed said. "We'll have to see about—"

"It's non-negotiable," Paul said. "Mom says I need to get a good night's sleep so I'm fresh for the test." He looked at his mother. "Right?"

Everyone looked at Paul's Mom. She raised one eyebrow and nodded. Her mouth formed just the hint of a smirk.

"Fine," Mr. Creed said. "We'll work on the date of the debate. What do you say, Paul? You want to be our next President?"

Paul looked at his mother again. "Can I, Mom? Pleeeeease?"

She put her hands on her hips. "You can't even keep your room clean, how are you going to run the country?"

"I'll make my bed every day for a year! I promise."

She turned to Mr. Creed. "Be straight with us. What makes you think this can work?"

"I'll be better than straight," he said. "I'll be blunt. It can work because people in this country are morons. Sixty-five percent of sports fans think the referees have rigged the game against their favorite team. Seventy-seven percent of Americans think angels are real. Do you know how many men think women's sole purpose on Earth is simply to make men squirm?"

"Wait, that last one's true, isn't it?" Artie said. Sylvia punched him on the arm.

"Fact is, you don't need to be a great statesman to win the Presidency," Mr. Creed said. "You just have to be unique enough to pique the interest of the American voters. I believe Paul fits that bill. He can win."

"No, you misunderstand me," Paul's Mom said. "I'm not asking whether he can win. I'm asking whether he could possibly do the job? He's only fifteen years old."

"Have you been paying attention to who's been in the White House for the past year?" Mr. Creed shared a look with the hot-looking reporter. "Don't worry, we'll surround him with people who know what they're doing. Country'd be no worse off than it already is."

Paul's Mom and Dad went off in a corner to debate privately. After ten or fifteen minutes they came back. "All right," Paul's Mom said. "As long as he gets all his schoolwork done. But he has to eat right and get to bed at a reasonable hour."

"Agreed." Mr. Creed shook their hands and then gave Paul a high-five. "Congratulations, Mr. Urbina-Pedisich. I'll make my recommendation in the morning. By Monday, I'm fairly sure you'll be the Democratic nominee for President of United States. In the meantime, we'll have to give some thought to who to tap for Vice President."

"Can I pick?" Paul said. "Please?"

Mr. Creed stared at Paul for a long time. "I suppose so. So long as it balances the ticket, helps us with a different demographic. And isn't Alison Denton."

Paul turned to Sylvia. He took hold of both her hands. "Sylvia Humphries, will you be my Vice President?"

Her answering smile lit the universe. Paul couldn't wipe off his stupid grin as he stared into her fathomless brown eyes. He felt warm all over.

He didn't notice the cold, dark storm clouds that swirled across Artie's face.

Twenty-one

They set up across the street from Independence Hall, in Old City Philadelphia, not far from the Liberty Bell. The square was packed for the introduction of the newly-minted Democratic nominee for President of the United States. Party officials, well-wishers, and the genuinely curious, seeking to witness history in the making.

The nominee stood about twenty feet from the stage, conferring with his campaign manager. Kayla Schwarzenegger stood with them as well, having been granted exclusive access as official chronicler of the nominee's non-public moments for the duration of the campaign. Her editor had gone faint when she told him the news.

The boy looked out at the thousands that had packed into the square. He looked at the jugglers and people dressed in colonial garb entertaining along the perimeter, the gigantic speakers, the plethora of blue and white signs with his name in big capital letters. He giggled.

"Now, don't be nervous, son," Lincoln Creed said. "Just do it like we practiced."

The boy didn't look nervous. He looked even younger than he was, maybe nine or ten, seeing the presents under the tree on Christmas morning. He giggled again.

Creed handed the lad a pair of horn-rimmed glasses, along with an encouraging nod.

Paul turned them over in his hand. Whoever had dressed him had gone middle-school-yearbook-photo standard. His mother had combed his hair again. "But I don't need glasses," he said.

"Put 'em on."

Creed gestured for the music, an old Huey Lewis song, which the campaign had chosen without the artist's permission.

It's hip to be square...

The crowd, a healthy percentage of whom weren't alive when the song was recorded, went bananas. Paul donned his new eyewear.

Kayla signaled for lights and a rolling camera. She began her interview, which her employer had agreed to air on whichever stations had offered them money.

"I'm here with Paul Urbina-Pedisich," Kayla said. "The first person under the voting age to ever be nominated for national office. Tell me, how does that feel?"

Hundreds of people crowded around, anxious to hear the Democratic candidate's first public statement. The flash from phones and cameras glinted off Paul's new glasses.

"It feels great," he said.

Those close enough to hear him gave out a huge cheer. A group of young women raised their arms over their heads and jiggled from side to side. Paul's hand covered the pimples on that side of his face and gave them a shy smile.

"You're about to speak to the American people for the first time," Kayla said. "What do you have to say to them? What's your message?"

"My message is we have a lot in common," Paul said. "Every single voter in the country was my age once. We understand each other."

"It's a big step, running for President of the United States. Have you ever run for office in a club, or at school?"

"Nah." The kid waved to two bra-less wonders who were jumping up and down and screaming his name. "Those things are all just popularity contests."

*　　　　*　　　　*

The local brigade of the LCPVM gathered at the mustering spot, inside the Stars-and-Stripes Tavern. The network had interrupted a re-run of *Kevin Can Wait* to air the introductory remarks of the Democratic candidate for President, much to the displeasure of the brigade.

Heath Dunbar wasn't grumbling like the others; he was a little bit excited. The candidate was eight years younger than Heath, but closer to his age than any other candidate, ever. And though Heath had never voted for a Democrat in his life, he felt a kind of kinship with Paul Urbina-Pedisich, a kind of pride. Heath was sure he wouldn't have been able to get around all those reporter's questions without tripping over his own tongue.

"What about guns in schools?" the reporter asked.

The brigade's collective ears perked up.

"Not in my school," Urbina-Pedisich said.

The brigade booed.

"You don't think teachers should be allowed guns to deal with dangerous situations?"

"Honestly, I don't think *anyone* should be allowed guns to deal with anything," the kid said. "But it's not my call, is it? I mean, the Second Amendment is what it is, it's part of the Constitution, we can't do anything about that. But my American History teacher told us the United States has more gun deaths per capita than Libya, Egypt, Sudan, and Israel *combined*. That's totally crazy, right? If it were up to me, I'd take a hard look at the words 'well regulated' in the Second Amendment. But please, don't put guns in my school and don't expand gun rights any further than the Constitution says."

The kid turned to someone off-camera and whispered, "Was that answer OK?"

The Colonel aimed the remote and silenced the television with a vicious twist of his wrist. "He can have my gun when he pries it from my cold, dead... whatever."

"I'm not sure that's what he meant, sir," Heath said. "I thought he was talking about reasonable restrictions, like we have for all the other amendments. Our First Amendment freedoms don't include death threats, or shouting 'fire' in a public theater. Is it really unreasonable to treat our Second Amendment freedoms the same way?"

"Latrine duty, Dunbar. Now." The Colonel pointed toward the door. "I'm calling the General. It's time to act, time to stand up for our rights." He glared at the cold, dead screen of the television. "Crisis like this demands an emergency response."

Twenty-two

The now former-President Passant left the White House that morning. Some staff stayed on with Acting-President O'Brien, but most non-essentials got their walking papers. Stanton was now working on the Passant campaign. He took along his former assistant chief-of-staff Craig, his former press liaison Stephanie, plus of course his yoga instructor. President Passant took along pretty much the entire circus that had carried him through his campaign the year before.

They all sat in the big conference room in Passant Place for a strategy meeting, except instead of strategizing they were watching TV.

The little kid the Democrats had nominated for President was giving his first major address. "I'm the perfect guy to run against the establishment," the kid said. "Have you ever known a teenager to listen to an authority figure?"

"Wait a minute, he can't do that," President Passant said. "*I'm* the anti-establishment candidate."

"Sir, you're the President of the United States," Craig said. "Or you were until Friday. How much more establishment could you be?"

President Passant turned to look at Stanton's staffer. He cocked his head to one side, his eyes stretched with thought.

"You're fired," he said.

The kid on TV kept talking but President Passant stopped listening. He sifted through a stack of postcards that had grabbed his attention. He held one up to Stanton. "Look at that skin tone, you ever see anything like that? Clearly not human, if you ask me."

Stanton examined the postcard. "That's makeup, sir. It's Commander Data. From the TV show, Star Trek."

President Passant snatched back the card. "Doesn't matter, Stanton. They know things. Things about the new Democratic candidate." He waved a different card, with a picture of the sexy blonde cylon from Battlestar Gallactica. "Hell, they knew who the candidate would be before any of the news outlets. I tell you, this is real." He held up a sheaf of papers. "Here, I have the transcripts, see for yourself."

"It's Pig Latin, sir. I translated it on the fly."

"Humphf." President Passant handed the papers to Stew Cannon. "I'm sure you can see the value here."

Stew took the transcripts and placed them in a green file folder. "Leave no dirt unturned, I always say. Can we talk about the campaign now?"

"What's to talk about," President Passant said. "We'll do rallies in all the swing states plus a couple here in New York. That ought to take care of it, right? I mean, look at that brat we're running against. What is he, twelve?"

"Fifteen, sir," Maryanne Monday said. "We also have the debate in three weeks. We should probably schedule some prep time the week before."

"Are you kidding me?" President Passant said. "I'll wipe the floor with the punk, just like I did with Crooked Alison. I won all three of those debates without preparing, everybody said so. Why would I need any prep time now?"

Maryanne's eyes crinkled, perhaps remembering that "everybody" included only Brightbutt News and a campaign-sponsored internet poll. She shot a look at Stew, then at Stanton. She pasted a smile on her face.

"Exactly what I was thinking, Mr. President."

*　　　　　*　　　　　*

Seamus got out of prison that same Monday. His boss gave him a fake passport and a thousand dollars and wished him well.

They'd probably never see each other again.

Seamus stopped at a public library and perused an atlas, looking for destinations where he could begin his new life, free from the pressures and burdens of being a CIA assassin.

He fell asleep atop a map depicting the Caucasus region south of Russia.

When he woke up, he found he'd made a decision. And it wasn't to take up mercenary life in Azerbaijan. He wouldn't be leaving the country, after all. He'd stay right there in DC.

He exited the library, keeping one eye over his shoulder to make sure he wasn't followed. He was grateful to his former boss for everything he'd done, but the guy worked for a United States intelligence service, he couldn't be trusted. Seamus lay 50/50 odds on a double-cross. If it weren't for the fact that the intelligence community was so busy "following" the new election, odds would even be higher.

He ducked into the first Metro station he saw, waited until the commuter rush had ended then boarded a train out to Bethesda. He plunked himself down at a hotel bar where he was sure he wouldn't run into any off-duty spooks because nobody he knew would pay $8.50 for a Miller Lite. He sipped the tasteless brew and looked up at the television, on which the Democratic nominee for President of the United States was giving a speech. He recognized the candidate's face, he'd studied it enough before his fateful final mission. He was surprised to see the kid behind a podium, but not shocked. After all, Paul Urbina-Pedisich was the reason he'd decided not to leave the country.

Seamus had some unfinished business.

Twenty-three

For presidential candidate Paul Urbina-Pedisich, the next few weeks went by in a blur. With the exception of homework and taking care of Orville, plus a couple of LGBTQ meetings with Sylvia, he was forced to devote every waking hour from 3pm to 10pm to campaign matters.

This particular Wednesday was Paul's first day off in two weeks, though it was less a day off and more the scheduled date of a "Candidate at Home" segment hosted by up-and-coming news superstar Kayla Schwarzenegger. Still, Paul was grateful to have a few quiet minutes next to Sylvia in the back of John 86's car.

The Johns, who wore pants and sneakers when not attending meetings, acted as self-appointed bodyguards for Paul and Sylvia, keeping fellow students at bay during school hours and occasionally driving the candidates home after school when the DNC helicopter wasn't waiting for them on the football field.

John kept the car radio on a news station, though he usually listened to heavy metal music that sounded to Paul like someone throwing an entire kitchen off a twenty-foot cliff. The announcer stated that President Passant had named his son Prince as his running mate, and had guaranteed that the move locked up the youth vote for him. He also claimed the allegiance of every other significant minority group.

"Nobody likes young people, women, blacks, Mexicans, gays, gooks, or Packers fans more than I do, he announced on Fox and Friends. "They won't find a better friend than me." To emphasize his point, he sent seven consecutive tweets saying exactly the same thing.

Prince held a news conference, with his Dad looming directly behind him, in which he refused to answer questions or say anything at all, other than to opine that the public knew him well enough to dispense with the need for a vice-presidential debate.

Which meant Sylvia could take plenty of time to study for the big math test that week, a luxury Paul simply couldn't afford. Mr. Creed had been putting him through four hours of debate preparation per night for the past eight days, though the good news was Paul also received all the pizza he could eat.

"Sounds like you have a full plate," Sylvia said, as Paul carried both their backpacks from John's car, through his front door, and up the stairs to his room. "I think we should let Artie do next week's octopus interview on his own."

"Wait, isn't that another interview with Kayla?" Paul said.

At the mention of Kayla's name, Sylvia made a scrunchy face that Paul could not begin to interpret, other than to understand his life would be significantly easier if he could begin to interpret it.

"Yes," Sylvia said. "That's why we should let Artie do it. He seems out-of-sorts lately."

"Tell me about it," Paul said. "No idea what his problem is. It's not like *he's* running for President." He grasped his room's door handle, twisted, and pulled.

"Maybe *that's* what his problem is—"

A large pail plummeted down from on top of the doorframe, splattering a dark red substance all over the hall.

Sylvia yelped. "Is that *blood?*"

Paul wrinkled his nose to keep from breathing in the noxious odor. "Probably pig's blood," he said. "My brother's watched *Carrie*, like, a hundred times. It's his favorite movie, except for *The Exorcist*."

Sylvia gaped at him. "How old did you say he was?"

"My brother, or the evil spirit trapped inside him?"

They both flinched at the appearance of a cherubic figure that seemed to materialize out of nowhere.

"Be afraid. Be very afraid," the cherub said in a piping, ten-year-old soprano.

Paul aimed his bellow down the stairs. "Mom!"

Sylvia was still breathing hard when they got down to the kitchen. Her blood pressure didn't seem to be helped by the sight of Paul's Mom chopping some sort of meat with a long, sharp-edged cleaver.

"Mom, put that down," Paul said. "We have to talk about young Freddy Krueger, upstairs."

His mom kept cutting the meat. "Win or lose, I'll always be your mother, and thus you'll *never* be my commander-in-chief. You want anything from me, a 'please' is going to play a major role."

Paul rolled his eyes. "Okay, Mom. Could you *please* put the cleaver down? You're making the future Vice President of the United States very nervous."

The doorbell rang. Paul ran to get it before his brother could answer the door decked out with his hockey mask and machete. Sylvia followed him into the foyer.

"Oh, hi Kayla." Paul tried to ignore the same uninterpretable scrunchy face from Sylvia. "Come on in."

Kayla waved in her sound and light crew. "Hi, kids. Where does your mother want us to set up, Paul?"

"I guess the kitchen," Paul said. "She's working on something in there."

"Oh?"

"Best not to ask," Sylvia said. "It's possible she's disposing of bodies."

Kayla walked rapidly ahead to consult with Paul's Mom. A few minutes later, the lights and microphones were all set up. Paul and Sylvia joined the others just as Kayla gave her introduction and asked Paul's Mom her first question, something about Paul's past success as a student. Paul looked at Sylvia and rolled his eyes again.

His mom saw. "Would you mind if Paul unloads the dishwasher while we talk?" she asked Kayla. "He was *supposed* to do that yesterday instead of hobnobbing with the French Ambassador."

Sylvia laughed. Paul's cheeks went hot. He tried not to grumble too loudly while he put away the dishes.

"Up until now, Paul's been a model student," his mom said. "He also plays fourth board on the chess team, and last year he did pretty well on the debate team. Debate starts up again soon, but sadly I don't think he'll be able to do it this year. Running for President has been a lot more time-consuming than we'd realized, though thankfully it's not as big a time commitment as our younger son has with travel soccer."

"Has the campaign interfered with Paul's school work?" Kayla said.

"He better hope not." His mom gave one of her chilling mom-smiles. "But like everything, it's a balance. If nothing else, we're hoping this running-for-president thing will look good on his college applications."

She turned toward Paul. "You know the Tupperware doesn't belong out on the counter, young man. The cabinet's right over there. And when you're done with that, the garbage can't get outside by itself."

The phone rang. Paul leapt for it before his mother could give him anything else to do. "Hello? Yes this Paul Urbina-Pedisich. Oh, hi, Ms. Stahl." He covered the mouthpiece and looked toward the others. "I'm sorry, but I have to take this."

"Oh, no you don't," his mom said. "You do your chores and then you can play with your friends at Sixty Minutes."

"Come on, Mom. If I become President, are you still going to make me do my chores?"

"It's good for you," she said.

"Actually," Kayla said. "The White House has dozens of people on staff whose job it is to perform these sorts of household functions. Nobody in the First Family does chores."

Paul's face lit up. He gave Sylvia a fist bump and his mom a smug little grin.

"Now I *really* want to win," he said.

Twenty-four

The morning of the only presidential debate of the campaign dawned gray and overcast. Paul greeted the day by trudging out to the bus stop. Edward N. Passant commemorated the occasion with a tweet.

 Edward N. Passant

@realEdwardNPassant

Will tonight's debate go past "Punky Pablo's" bedtime? Hope the people at Penn stock juice boxes!

5:21 AM - 16 Nov 2017

Paul left school early for a final prep session. Sylvia came outside to wait with him for the limo. "I'm bringing our friends from the meeting," she said. Paul's eyes may have bulged a little.

"Don't worry, they'll all be wearing pants. Nobody will know who they are." She got up on tiptoes and gave him a kiss on the cheek. "I'll be cheering for you," she said.

The car came and Paul climbed into the back. The trip to the Annenberg Theater on the campus of the University of Pennsylvania, where the debate would be held that evening, was not a long one, but Paul couldn't quell the queasy feeling in his stomach. He hadn't had one in a long time, but he actually wouldn't have minded a juice box.

The driver, who was a real Secret Service agent, led him into a building next to the theater and left him with his campaign manager. Paul slung his backpack — which like the backpack of every other high school student he knew, weighed upwards of 225 pounds — onto the back of a chair, which promptly collapsed. Mr. Creed glanced up for a moment then went back to the financial report or whatever he was studying.

Paul held up his phone to display his Twitter feed. "Why does he call me 'Punky Pablo'?"

"It's like 'Lyin' Ned' or 'Crooked Alison.'" Mr. Creed didn't look up. "If it catches on, then your name itself takes on a negative connotation."

"But my name isn't 'Pablo.' Why not say 'Punky Paul' or 'Punky PUP'?" That last one, a play on his initials, actually sounded pretty cool. He might try to spread it himself, maybe give him a little cred in the cafeteria.

Mr. Creed put down his report and picked up something off the news wire. "Don't worry about it. Calling you 'Pablo' might make people believe you're Hispanic without him sounding overtly racist. At least that's what he's shooting for."

"But that's true. I'm really into my family tree, you know? I did the full treatment on Ancestry.com and everything. My great-grandfather immigrated here from Spain in the nineteen-thirties. So I *am* part Hispanic."

"You got a lot to learn, kid. This is a presidential campaign. The *last* thing that matters is what's true." Mr. Creed finally looked up. "Now let's finish up your answer on NATO, then we'll do one last practice session in the auditorium."

*   *   *

The big press room behind the stage was buzzing, about a half hour before the candidates would take the stage. Every network was broadcasting its pre-show, live, and Kayla drank it all in. On the right-hand side of the room, Maryanne Monday was offering some Grade A spin to Sam Hattery. "That's what people misunderstand," she said. "That's what they have wrong. The alternative fact is, President Passant was trying to *protect* the boy, that's why he brought in a government operative, to make sure nothing bad happened. And he was successful, the boy was unharmed. We should all be thankful. This is just the biased press being unfair again."

On the opposite side of the room, an MSNBC panelist said, "It's shaping up to be an epic clash of two visions for America."

Another panelist snorted. "Two *blurry* visions, you mean. On the one hand, a kid who looks like he hasn't finished puberty yet, who's given maybe three public speeches in his life, and on the other hand, Edward N. Passant, who's either been President or running for President for the past two and a half years and other than himself I still have no idea what he stands for."

"You bring up a good point," the first panelist said. "One candidate is fifteen years old and the other is President Passant. Which do you think will exhibit more maturity during the debate tonight?"

They all began babbling simultaneously.

In the corner, a scar-faced man in an expensive Italian suit and slicked-back hair caught Kayla's attention. Another man, thin with prematurely white hair, slunk over to the first and surreptitiously transferred something, receiving a small slip of paper in return. The white-haired man turned toward Kayla and she recognized Henderson Hooper, from CNN.

"Who's that guy you were just talking to?" she asked Hooper.

"Who, Benny Bagodonuts? He runs the backstage betting at these things." He glanced at his slip of paper. "I took the kid plus five percentage points. Pretty good odds, I'd say. Didn't want to miss out on that action." He stuffed the paper into his pocket. "Personally, I think the over/under on 'believe me' is too high. I'll probably go with the under. But I'm definitely taking the over on how many times Passant mentions his net worth."

The bell chimed, signifying the event was about to start. Kayla wandered over to the left wing to stand with Lincoln Creed. The candidates walked out and shook hands. President Passant adjusted his grip and gave Paul the classic sixth grade "bone crusher" handshake. He smirked on his way to his podium, while Paul flexed his arm to regain feeling in his fingers. Andrea Robinson took her place as moderator of the debate.

"Good evening from the campus of the University of Pennsylvania, in Philadelphia, PA," she said. "I'm Andrea Robinson, from NBC Nightly News, and I'd like to welcome you to the only presidential debate of this special election."

Marlena and the various Passant children sat in the front row on one side, with a group behind them who looked like they'd come straight from Wall Street but were probably actors.

Kayla thought she recognized a few faces from the fake press pen at Passant's stadium speeches. Behind Paul's parents on the other side, it looked like a high school pep rally, complete with at least two cheerleaders.

Andrea went on. "This ninety-minute debate is sponsored by the Commission on Presidential Debates, which drafted tonight's format and agreed to the rules with both campaigns. I have chosen the questions, but have not shared them with either the commission or the campaigns. Each candidate will have up to two minutes to respond to each question, after which I may ask follow-up questions or allow open discussion. The audience has agreed to remain silent throughout the debate so we can focus on what the candidates are saying."

Paul had lowered his microphone as much as possible, but when he slouched he still could've rested his chin on it. The audience could see his face and the top of his shoulders but that was about it. His eyes seemed slightly glazed; if he'd nibbled his lip any harder he'd have bled all over his clip-on tie.

Edward Passant regarded his opponent with a stern expression, attempting to walk the fine line between reminding the viewing public of the absurdity of a child sharing the stage with a past President and reminding them of an abusive parent after one too many Scotch-and-Sodas.

"I will invite you to applaud now, however," Andrea said. "To welcome the candidates: Democratic nominee, Paul Urbina-Pedisich, and Republican nominee, Edward N. Passant."

The Wall Street side clapped heartily. The pep rally gang went berserk. Andrea Robinson held up one hand. "Thank you. The first question is for Mr. Urbina-Pedisich, and let's start with the elephant in the room. You're fifteen years old, why do you think you're capable of being President of the United States?"

"Elephant?" Passant said. "More like the dinosaur in the room. Not one of those velociraptors, either, not a cool, big-league carnivore. No, one of those slow, blundering plant-eaters, maybe a brontosaurus. Fifty thousand pounds, with the brain the size of a walnut, very small brain. That's what this is. Kind of like Congress, all those politicians. I had great policy, great. But they wouldn't pass the legislation I wanted. Everybody agreed the country would have been better off with my ideas, believe me. No doubt about that. Who could do it better than me? I built a truly great company, tremendous. I had a big income, huge! I built a great country, too. I think I did a very good job. What's *he* done?" He pointed at Paul. "Worked a paper route?"

"Excuse me, President Passant," Andrea said. "But the question was for Mr. Urbina-Pedisich."

Passant glowered. He'd also pushed his microphone down; he had to hunch and bend forward to speak into it. "You asked about the Presidency. I think I had a right to speak."

"Mr. Urbina-Pedisich?" Andrea said.

"Thank you, Ms. Robinson, that's a really good question." Paul turned to look at Creed, who gave him an approving nod. "I think my best attribute is my perspective. Like on the environment and global warming and stuff. I'll be breathing the air and drinking the water long after my opponent is pushing up daisies. I understand the crushing burden of college tuition on young people in middle-class families, I worry more about things like social security disappearing and the national debt, because my generation will have to pay it back."

"You should worry more about your mom docking your allowance, if you keep giving answers like that," Passant said.

"President Passant, you already took your turn," Andrea said. "But since you're so anxious to speak, let's move on to the next question, which is for you. One of your first acts in office was to defund Planned Parenthood. What do you have to say to the millions of women whose health was affected by that decision?"

"Abortion?" Kayla said to Creed. "That's a big gun for Andrea to bring out so early."

"That's why we love her," Creed said.

Passant pointed at the camera. "Look, health care was a mess before I got here, such a mess. But I fixed it, everyone says our plan was a great success. Or it would have been if they'd passed it. The only people who don't say that are the dishonest media. Look at Ohio, look at Michigan, look at North Carolina. They've all introduced legislation to make abortion illegal. Which I agree with, because I support swing states. That's why I win, why I appointed that guy from Colorado to the Supreme Court. After that, it was only a matter of time before the Court outlawed Planned Parenthood anyway, believe me. I did everyone a favor."

"Mr. Urbina-Pedisich, would you like to respond?"

"Sure, Ms. Robinson. I disagree. Especially the part where President Passant said he favors making abortion illegal. I would never, ever tell a woman she's breaking the law by choosing what to do with her own body. If I told my Mom that, she'd ground me for a week, and I'd deserve it."

Passant hunched and leaned forward. "I never said that."

"Dude, you said it, like, two minutes ago."

"That's disgraceful, the way he's talking to me." Passant's expression went from stern to menacing. "Very disgraceful. Someone ought to wash his mouth out with soap."

Paul took his microphone and stepped away from the podium. Creed nodded and smiled.

"Can I say something else?" Paul said. "Seems to me a lot of the people who are against abortion are also against birth control. That's crazy, right? I mean, hey, you gotta give me one or the other."

"I'm sorry," Andrea said. "Are you saying you're in favor of pre-marital sex?"

"You ever meet a teenage male who wasn't?"

Paul extended his microphone arm and crooked his other elbow, dipping his head as if about to sneeze into his sleeve.

Kayla gaped. "Did the Democratic nominee just *dab* at a presidential debate?"

"Bet your ass he did," Creed said.

Twenty-five

Stanton Young paced back and forth in the right wing of the stage. Before the debate, he'd convinced himself President Passant would have learned from his disastrous three debates against Alison Denton the year before. He was paying the price for that bit of self-delusion now. His ulcers were flaring worse than ever but all he could do was stand there and watch it coming, like an oncoming train.

"In my first year, I lowered the deficit more than any other president in the history of our country," President Passant said. "That's nine months for us versus four years, or very often eight years, for the others. I'm very proud of it. Biggest reduction in history."

"Uh, excuse me," Andrea Robinson said. "But according to the latest OMB reports, the deficit went *up* during your time in office, by more than a trillion dollars."

"Wrong," President Passant said. "Biggest. Reduction. Ever. Next question."

Maryanne Monday sprinted away to the spin room, to make desperate calls to whatever conservative economists she could find at this hour and try to figure out some new way to recalculate the deficit.

The mediator compounded things by tossing the kid the softball of what he would do if he became President. Stanton focused on his own candidate's face, hoping beyond hope he'd cease to scowl like a black-hat professional wrestler.

"I'll tell you what I *won't* do, Ms. Robinson," the kid said. "I won't appoint a Bizarro World cabinet like President Passant did. You know, where everything is backward? I won't appoint a guy whose life's work has been breaking unions and opposing the minimum wage as Secretary of Labor…"

President Passant hunched and leaned toward his microphone. "Wrong."

"…or a climate-change denier as head of the Environmental Protection Agency, which my Biology teacher, Mr. Harrison, says we should now call the Environmental *Destruction* Agency. I won't hire a xenophobic National Security Advisor, or a Housing and Urban Development Secretary who's opposed to public housing…"

The air raid siren went off in Stanton's pocket.

"Shit! Who let the President have his phone?" He turned to the only aide he had left, since Craig had been fired. "Stephanie, wasn't it your job to confiscate President Passant's phone?"

"Yes, sir, but he wouldn't give it to me. I made a grab for it, until the Secret Service stepped in."

Stanton read the tweet. He sighed.

Edward N. Passant

@realEdwardNPassant

Punky Pablo's third-rate teacher, @MrHarrison, has done a terrible job. No wonder public education is such a mess!

9:08 PM - 16 Nov 2017

"I guess you did your best. Go show this to Maryanne so she can get the spin machine rolling on this one. She's going to have to dig up something on this Mr. Harrison before he starts giving interviews on CNN." He watched Stephanie run off, ignoring the sharp pains in his chest.

The kid was still talking. "I got an A is Social Studies last year and I have an A-minus in AP American History. Though I'm hoping to bring it up to an A with some extra credit. I've read the Constitution and everything. The whole thing, even the amendments."

Andrea Robinson smiled at the boy, then turned to the alleged adult on the stage. "That brings up an interesting point, President Passant. Have *you* ever read the Constitution?"

President Passant grabbed his microphone and started pacing the stage while he spoke, toward the kid then away then toward again, circling closer and closer.

"Small thinking, Andrea. I've done *better* than read the Constitution. I've envisioned its future. That's what I do, what I've always done in business. I have a very big corporation, lots of profit. I buy a lot of companies. And when I purchase a new subsidiary, usually a competitor of mine that I've beaten and dismantled…"

On the word "beaten" his teeth got dangerously close to the kid's ear. Then he swerved away. If they started playing the theme from Jaws, nobody would have blinked.

"Out with the old, in with the new, that's how I've become one of the richest men in the world. I happen to think I'm the richest, but we can say 'one of,' for now. I have a plan to upgrade the Constitution, believe me. I can't reveal it here, that's just what ISIS wants, but I will tell you this, it'll be a beautiful thing. We'll have a document that will make America proud again, that will make America safe again, and that will make America *great* again."

Daniel and Edward, Jr., Isabel and her husband, and the 27 actors they hired all clapped and cheered, until Andrea Robinson gave them the eye.

The kid gave a classic teenager smirk. "I guess we should take that as a 'no,' then?"

President Passant's face flushed bright red. His left hand formed a fist. "Listen punk, you're the snot-nosed little twerp whose lunch money I used to take at recess, right before I stuffed you into your locker."

He stepped toward the kid, who ducked back and cowered behind his podium.

This time, nobody clapped.

Twenty-six

The mood behind the stage on which President Edward N. Passant was speaking the next day to the adoring masses could best be described as jovial, except for Stanton, of course, who couldn't have been best described as jovial since he was a toddler.

President Passant, on the other hand, was never happier than when he was speaking to 20,000 people who were already voting for him. And if he was happy, his staff was under strict orders to be happy as well, or else.

"They're trying to use a rigged system to take the Presidency away from *you*, the People," President Passant declared. "What do we say to that?"

"TAKE IT BACK! TAKE IT BACK!"

It was a cloudy Friday night in Staten Island, in a state President Passant had zero chance to carry, but he had insisted, primarily because his club at Mar-a-Loogie was under renovations. He swaggered off the stage to thundering applause while already checking his phone.

"Where does fake news CNN get off saying I lost the debate?" he said the moment his mike was turned off. "I won the debate, hands down. Everyone I talk to says I won it. Everyone."

"Yes, sir," Stanton said. "But they all work for you."

President Passant held up his phone so Stanton could see a particular tweet. "More importantly, what are we doing about this?"

 Orville the Octopus

@OrvilleSays

Orville doesn't like bullies, @realEdwardNPassant

11:17 AM - 17 Nov 2017

Stanton's shoulders sagged. "Sir, do we really want to start a tweet storm over an invertebrate with two hundred followers?"

The joviality in the atmosphere evaporated quickly. "If that thing isn't on a platter in one of my restaurants by the close of business tomorrow, I swear all your heads will be. Now, get me out of here."

The group of them trooped into the limo, President Passant, Maryanne Monday, Stew Cannon and the assistant he'd brought over from Brightbutt News, Stanton and his aide Stephanie. There wasn't room for Stanton's yoga instructor.

President Passant got right to it. "This is bigger than a lousy octopus. The lying media keeps calling me a bully. It's everywhere. I don't get it. Last election, they didn't make such a fuss when I beat up on a woman, did they? Why now? We can't let this go, we need to hit back, ten times harder." He turned to Stanton's aide Stephanie. "What do you think, Cecily? Am I a bully? And let me remind you your job depends on your answer."

"It's Stephanie, sir..."

"Whatever."

"...and of course I don't think, I mean, I wouldn't characterize, that is—"

Stanton came to her rescue. "Mr. President, we have more important things to discuss than who thinks who is a bully." He pulled a sheaf of papers from his briefcase.

"That better not be polling data," President Passant said. "Everyone knows the polls are rigged. Every poll said I was going to lose last time, remember? But I won. Biggest margin ever. Polls are completely useless." He poured himself a Scotch from the limo's stash, offering one to Stew but nobody else. "Unless this poll has me leading?"

"It's not polls that worry me, so much as demographics," Stanton said. "Take this seriously, sir. We could have a real problem."

"The kid's running the same namby-pamby platform as Alison Denton did," President Passant said. "Our supporters haven't changed their stripes, they'll never go for all that inclusion or 'stronger together' nonsense. They'll vote for me no matter what, I can show you—"

"Mr. President, please don't shoot someone on Fifth Avenue just to prove a point. And it's not our supporters that concern me, it's Urbina-Pedisich's. It's really a matter of turnout."

"Don't worry about turnout. That's what won us the last election."

"Again, sir, not *our* turnout. The boy's. Specifically, I'm worried about the youth vote. There are over fifty million registered voters between the ages of eighteen and twenty-nine. Less than half of them voted last time, and Denton had a ten million vote margin."

"That age group never turns out," Stew Cannon's assistant said.

"When's the last time they had a teenager to vote for?" Stephanie said.

The assistant began frantically researching on his phone.

"It was a rhetorical question."

"Let's hypothesize for a moment," Stanton said. "Forty-some percent of them turned out last year, but what if the kid energizes youth voters like we've never seen? What if eighty or ninety percent of them turn out this time? Assuming the same ratio votes Democratic — and that's a dangerous assumption, it could easily be much worse — that would give Urbina-Pedisich *thirty million* more votes than Denton had, spread out all over the country. It would make our electoral map look like Goldwater's." He met each of their eyes, ending with President Passant.

"If it happens, we can't win, Mr. President. We won't even come close."

Maryanne's brow crinkled. Stew's eyes narrowed as the conniving gears in his head ground against each other. Stephanie nodded thoughtfully.

"Means we have to find a way to depress youth turnout," she said. "How's the best way to do that?"

Stew's assistant scratched his head. "That another rhetorical question?"

Nobody responded. They all sat, deep in thought, until they arrived at Passant Place. President Passant spent the entire time looking at Stephanie.

The car stopped. President Passant seemed to arrive at some decision. "Stephanie, could you come upstairs for a few moments. I'd like you to help me with something."

He popped a tic-tac into his mouth.

Twenty-seven

Presidential candidate Paul Urbina-Pedisich loitered in the hallway by the pre-engineering classrooms, enjoying the fuss two senior girls made over him. Both wore freshly printed "Gotta give me one or the other" tee-shirts. He wasn't sure how to tell for certain, but he didn't think the one on the left was wearing a bra.

Sylvia skipped up to them. She was always skipping wherever she went. She tapped him on the shoulder.

"Oh, hi," he said, before returning his attention to his future constituents.

"You heading over to the Bio lab?" Sylvia said. "It's Orville time."

Paul didn't turn away from the senior girls. "I don't think I have time today."

Sylvia stamped her foot. She was wearing some sort of clog that made a clunky sound against the floor. "Seriously? It's your turn. You promised Artie."

"You do it."

She reached out and turned his chin so he faced her. "You took on the responsibility, Paul, nobody forced you to volunteer."

He yanked away. "Now you sound like my mother. Trust me, I get enough of that at home. You're getting kinda tedious." He deliberately turned his back on her.

Her tone changed, got lower and flatter. Perhaps if Paul could have seen her eyes he would have recognized the warning signs. "Well, if that's the way you want it."

Paul's neck reddened with annoyance. "Yeah, that's the way I want it."

"I'm very disappointed in you," she said, while his breathing quickened. "I never thought you'd let your friends down like this. I never thought you'd be such a—"

"Listen up." He spun around, teeth bared, practically shouting. "I'm going to be President of the United States. The United States, understand? I'm going to be the boss of the whole country." His entire face was bright red now, he could feel the heat in his cheeks and forehead. "You really think I have time for a stupid *octopus*?"

He stalked away. Sylvia stormed off in the opposite direction.

"Fine," she snarled over her shoulder. "Have it your way."

"I will!"

About halfway down the hall, Paul felt really stupid.

He beat back the feeling. He *was* going to be President of the United States. Or, even if he lost the election he'd still be a very important person. And she was just a dumb girl who didn't know what she was talking about.

"Right?" he said, but there was nobody around him to answer.

*   *   *

Kayla Schwarzenegger was on a roll. Seemed like everything she touched turned to headlines. Her editor had basically given her carte blanche. Write whatever and whenever she wished, travel wherever on the paper's dime, follow any impulse or hunch she happened to dream up. It was almost like he worked for her and not the other way around. The job offers were rolling in, though she wouldn't have time or energy to deal with them until after the election. She'd become a frequent guest panelist on CNN and MSNBC, and her new friend Andrea Robinson had Kayla on her show at least once a week. Including today, to critique the previous day's debate and that day's Passant rally.

The latest octopus tweet had been rather serendipitous. She was finally interviewing the creature and its handlers the following Monday. But today, already in New York, a mere eight blocks from Passant Place, she could hop a cab and maybe get a reaction from the Passant campaign. Maybe from Edward Passant, himself, though she wasn't sure she could face him after what he'd done to her at that fateful press conference that seemed a million years ago.

Her segment lasted an hour after the Staten Island rally ended, most of the time spent debating who loved Passant more, his fans or himself? She wasn't sure how long it would take the Republican entourage to get back to the Place, but probably long enough that she could get hold of someone fairly high up in the campaign before they dispersed.

The cab ride was quick. Passant's private security guys manned the Place entrance, which meant the posse had already arrived. Kayla flashed her press credentials at them and breezed into the lobby. She was about to push the elevator button when she noticed a young blonde woman sitting on the edge of a large planter, with her head in her hands. She walked toward her, having recognized the woman as one of Stanton Young's aides. At best, she might get a juicy quote; at the very least she should be able to ferret out who'd be available upstairs.

"Hi," she said. "I'm Kayla Schwarzenegger, of the Philadelphia Inquirer. I was wondering if you had a minute to answer a couple quick questions?"

The woman flinched at the sound of Kayla's voice. She raised her head, revealing red-rimmed eyes and streaked makeup. "What?"

Kayla sat down next to her. "What happened?"

"Nothing." The woman covered her face again.

"Look at me." Kayla waited patiently for the woman to comply. She gazed into her bloodshot eyes for a long moment. "I've seen that look before," Kayla said. "In the mirror. Who did this to you?"

"Nobody. I can't tell you."

"That's fine. You don't have to say who." Didn't matter, there was no shortage of creep-bastards in the Passant campaign, starting right at the top. "What's your name?"

"Stephanie."

Did he hurt you, Stephanie?"

"No. It's so stupid, I can't believe I'm making such a fuss over it. All he did was lean into me and kiss me, in the elevator. On the lips." She absently wiped her mouth. "That's not such a big deal, right?"

Kayla softened her voice as much as she could. "Wrong. It is a big deal."

"It was probably my fault. I must have done something to lead him on."

"You know it wasn't, and you didn't," Kayla said. "That reaction is exactly how his sort of person gets away with it."

"Best just to forget about it."

All Kayla could do was shrug. How could she tell this woman to stand up for herself when Kayla had done no such thing in the exact same circumstance?

"Can I help you get home, Stephanie?"

The young woman nodded. Kayla helped her outside and into a cab. On an impulse, she got in with her. "Let me just make sure you get there," she said.

Stephanie thanked her, then covered her face again while her whole body shook. "I can't believe it's getting to me like this," she said. "It really was nothing."

"That's what I thought, too," Kayla said.

They arrived at the woman's address and Kayla walked her up to her apartment. She told Stephanie the story of her own "nothing."

The young woman's eyes widened when Kayla told her the name of the man who had pawed at her. Didn't take finely honed deductive skills to guess who Stephanie was protecting. She flopped onto a sofa and started to cry again. "I always looked up to him," she said, so faintly Kayla could barely hear.

Kayla gave Stephanie a hug. She knew the woman would never say anything. Never confront the man, never out him to the world. Kayla couldn't blame her.

He would get away with it. Again. There was nothing Kayla could do to help this poor young woman.

Stephanie clung to Kayla, sobbing. Then she stopped, leaned back. "Thank you so much. I'm OK now."

It struck Kayla all at once. "No, thank *you*," she said.

There *was* one thing she could do.

Twenty-eight

Stanton hobbled into the small conference room at Passant Place about 8am the next day. He didn't think there was anything physically wrong with him, and yet all his joints felt stiff and achy. Stephanie giving notice that morning had brought this on. She said she'd gotten a better job opportunity, as a circus barker in her home town of Milwaukee. To Stanton, it didn't sound much different than what she'd done on the campaign, but what did he know?

The only other person in the room was Stew Cannon, banging away on his laptop, surrounded by crumpled papers. Stanton felt like he was alone on an island with one of those creepy clowns you see in horror movies. Stew didn't acknowledge Stanton's presence, but every so often he would chuckle maniacally.

Their boss strode into the room, followed by Maryanne Monday. "OK, people," President Passant said. "Where are we on the octopus?"

Stanton sagged in his chair. "Excuse me, sir. You mean, where are we on suppressing youth turnout, don't you?"

President Passant glared at him for a full minute.

"OK, the octopus," Stanton said. "It apparently lives in a suburb of Philadelphia. We're running it down, but it appears there's some connection to Paul Urbina-Pedisich."

President Passant banged on the table with his fist. "Damn. I *knew* we should have taken care of that kid when we had the chance." He looked up at the others. "I mean, now what?"

"Good news." Stew held up a piece of paper. "The latest missive from our 'alien' friends has proven fruitful."

He gave a creepy-clown-holding-a-fourteen-inch-knife smile. "I know our next move."

*   *   *

Paul was joined at the breakfast table Saturday morning by his parents, his demon-spawn brother, and two Secret Service agents, who both had second helpings of pancakes. Since the day before the debate, the agents had gone with him everywhere, even home, where they stayed in the guest room, presumably after arm wrestling to see who got the bed and who had to sleep on the floor. The only place they didn't go was inside the school, because Paul's Mom had made them promise not to.

There was frost on the grass in the front yard. Paul's Mom bundled him up warm and led him to the family car to take him into Center City, where Paul was supposed to stop by at a retreat for freshmen in Congress. The Secret Service guys followed in a not-at-all-inconspicuous black government vehicle.

"I thought Sylvia was coming with us?" Paul's Mom said.

"Yeah, I don't know where she is. I called her but she didn't answer."

He tried to keep his tone even, but her mom-sense saw easily through his subterfuge. "Everything OK between you two?"

"What? Yeah, 'course." Paul took his phone out to check his Twitter feed. "I don't want to talk about it, OK?"

They got into the city, stopped in front of a really old, red brick and brownstone building on Broad Street. Mom said she'd go shopping and would see him in an hour. The Secret Service guys got out with Paul, leaving their not-at-all-inconspicuous black government vehicle double-parked in front of the building and snarling traffic all the way up to City Hall. A chorus of honks and rude shouts followed them up the sweeping staircase and into the building. Paul hoped the drivers weren't registered voters.

A butler in a conservative suit led them to a high-ceilinged ballroom, it's dark wood-paneled walls festooned with portraits of super-old, white men. The Secret Service agents took position on either side of the doorway. Fifty or sixty newly-minted senators and representatives stopped their conversations when Paul was announced. About half of them, who Paul figured were the Republicans, stared at him over wrinkled noses and flat mouths. The other half cheered. A youngish man with a name tag identifying him as the junior Senator from Delaware stepped forward and shook Paul's hand.

"Great to meet you," he said. "Would you like me to show you around?"

After the first few introductions, Paul realized he'd never remember anyone without staring ostentatiously at their name tags, so he decided to avoid saying anyone's name and catalog them internally by the state they were from. It got a little tricky when he met four different freshmen representatives from

California, but one was a woman, one was African-American, and one was Asian, so he was able to make it work.

It got fun after a while. The Democrats, at least, were happy to meet him, including several who suggested grabbing lunch, although not until after he was elected. Delaware went so far as to sneak Paul a glass of whiskey, from which Paul took one sip and nearly gagged. At his first opportunity, he dumped it into a big flowerpot in the corner. He half-expected the plant to whither on the spot.

His mother appeared in the doorway. Not ready to leave, Paul hid behind the California delegation, but somehow Mom materialized out of nowhere.

"Time to go, honey," she said. "You have a Biology test on Monday and I know you haven't finished your extra-credit paper on separation of powers. So say goodbye to your new friends." She kissed him on the top of his head.

"Mom!" Paul turned bright red. "Not in front of the other politicians."

He waved to everyone on his way out then he, his mom, and the Secret Service guys left the building and got into their cars. Paul secured his seatbelt then glanced at his 1400 unread emails before quickly going to shut off his phone. Mr. Creed would tell him if there was anything important.

Before he could power it down, his phone dinged. A text message. From Mr. Creed. Telling him something was important. Paul groaned.

Check Twitter, right now, the text said.

Oh, was that all? Paul brought up his Twitter app to check out the latest salvo from his sort-of-esteemed opponent.

His jaw dropped.

Edward N. Passant

@realEdwardNPassant

I'm hearing Punky Pablo attends LGBTQ meetings. Which is he? L? G? B? T? or Q?

3:36 PM - 18 Nov 2017

"What is it, honey?" his mother said.
"Nothing good, Mom. Nothing good."

Twenty-nine

Kayla worked all weekend on the article, made sure she got every fact straight, had every emotion contained. She did not want to come off as just another "hysterical woman." She'd chosen to go up against a sabre-tooth tiger and this was the one bullet in her gun.

She marched into her editor's office, first thing Monday morning.

"Is this about the LGBTQ thing?" he said. "Exactly the sort of thing where your access to the campaign gives us a huge advantage."

Kayla blinked. She'd been focusing on nothing but her article; she had no idea what he was talking about. "I'll get you something on that later today." She handed him her article. "Right now, I want to talk about this."

He glanced at the printout she'd handed him. His eyes popped out like they were connected by springs. He ran his fingers across the headline as though the letters might shift at his touch.

GROPED — MY CLOSE ENCOUNTER OF THE POTUS KIND

She'd never seen him do anything as quickly as he read through the article. When he was done, he said, "You have a really bright future, Kayla, you can write your own ticket. You sure you want to do this?"

"I am." She'd thought about nothing but that question for the past 48 hours. "I can handle the heat."

"Maybe. You might also become radioactive."

She didn't hesitate. "It's worth the risk. If you don't want to run it, I'm sure I can find someone who does."

"Are you kidding?" He clasped the article to his Tommy Hilfiger-covered chest. "Of course *I* want to run it. I'm just not sure you should."

"Run it," she said. "Post it on the website and put it in the paper tomorrow. I'm ready." She looked at her watch. "Now, if you don't mind, I have to go prepare for an interview with an octopus."

*   *   *

Paul hadn't seen Sylvia all day, but in true teenage-stalker fashion he loitered after school near her locker, a vantage from which he could see her but she was unlikely to see him, pretending to read a chapter on the Plenary Power Doctrine.

There she was, coming toward the locker, talking to some boy. Paul's hands curled into fists, but he made the effort to straighten them back out. Who cared what she did, anyway?

Soon as the other boy walked away toward his own locker, Paul beelined straight toward his running mate. Her dimples lit up when she saw him, but then she seemed to remember she was cross with him and she scrunched up her face. "What do *you* want?" she said.

Paul tried to match the flatness of her tone. "Did you do it?"

"What?"

"Did you tell them about me going to the meetings? I know you're mad at me, but—"

To Paul it seemed Sylvia burst into flame. "*What?* Do you really think I would do something like that? Do you think *anyone* in the group would do something like that? Well, guess what? While you were off gallivanting and ogling your constituents and asking insulting questions, the group decided to hold a special meeting to figure out what happened. Just for *you*, not that you deserve it." She checked the time. "It's right now. I'll let you come if you promise not to say anything. Especially not to me. And don't you *dare* ask anyone else if they 'did it.' Don't be even more of a jerk than I already think you are."

Paul's neck reddened but he remembered how sharp her fingernails were, so he chose not to speak. He followed her down the stairs to the room near the swimming pool and sat down next to her. With a "hmph," she got up and flopped into a chair as far away from him as possible. He gripped the arms of his own chair and glared at anyone who looked at him.

Which was everyone. Every expression reflected the pride and awe in the knowledge that their *friend* was a real-life candidate for President of the United States, mixed with the sorrow and shock and anger that someone in the room had betrayed him, really betrayed them all. Paul glared at each of them, but none of them appeared the slightest bit guilty. Was anybody absent, or was someone a super-good actor?

The group leader took attendance, something Paul had never seen her do before. She went through the entire list, announced that everyone who had been to a meeting that semester was present in the room. She opened the floor for discussion.

John 69 spoke first. "Our first rule is never to out one of our members or friends. Somebody broke that rule." With his hulking demeanor, menacing expression, and stiletto heels, he could have intimidated Darth Maul, maybe even Nancy Pelosi. "Whoever it was needs to speak up. *Now.* Don't compound your mistake by staying quiet."

Nobody spoke. Nobody moved. John bared his teeth in a grimace. "We are not leaving this room until the culprit identifies him or herself." He plunked hard into his seat and folded his massive arms in front of his chest to settle in for the wait.

Everyone looked at everybody else. Nobody said a word. After close to ten very uncomfortable minutes of silence, John 86 stood up, no less intimidating than John 69.

"Come on, people. Every single person who knew Paul has attended our meetings is in this room right now. It has to be one of us. I know I didn't do it, which means one of you did. We need to know who it was, for Paul's sake, and for the rest of us, too." He clamped his mouth shut but continued breathing very hard, which created a sort of hissing sound, like a pissed-off viper. "Don't let this get ugly."

More silence. No guilty faces. John's words echoed in Paul's head.

Every single person who knew Paul has attended our meetings is in this room right now. It has to be one of us.

Paul slapped his hand over his mouth. They'd all been working under the same assumption as John, but they'd all been wrong.

"I know who it was," Paul said.

Thirty

By 3pm, the Twitter frenzy was in full whirlwind mode. It had started before Kayla had even arrived home from the newsroom. Exhausted and disheveled after barely sleeping all weekend, she'd fumbled with the keys to her building, and her phone had dropped out of her purse. She bent and picked it up, but once it was in her hand, she couldn't resist checking to see if her article was up.

It was, along with a couple dozen comments. A few supportive, one lewd, but mostly hateful and spiteful. She wondered at that until she checked Twitter, where Edward Passant had already weighed in.

Edward N. Passant

@realEdwardNPassant

More FAKE NEWS. How could I have assaulted a woman I've never met? Shame on you, @KaylaS!

9:14 AM - 20 Nov 2017

After that, armed with Kayla's Twitter handle, the Passant supporters abandoned their usual social media vulgarity in favor of some serious spewing. The death threats and slut-shaming didn't bother her so much, but the suggestions that she be dismembered and urinated upon before getting gang-raped were a bit disconcerting. She'd left her editor's office an hour before, convinced she was prepared for all this. Now she wasn't so sure.

She went inside and showered, but the hot water couldn't wash away the filth being hurled at her. She put on some fresh clothes, fixed herself a light lunch, and prepared her questions for the octopus. She arrived at Lower Merion High School at 3pm.

Her phone rang, her editor checking up on her.

"Jeez," she said. "I had no idea you were so anxious for this octopus story. Sorry to disappoint, but I just got here so I haven't interviewed the old cephalopod yet. Don't worry, I'll let you know the minute I'm done with this soon-to-be award-winning piece."

Her editor wasn't in the mood for jocularity. "Have you seen Passant's tweet?"

"Yeah, he's never heard of me. Big surprise."

"No, the other one."

Kayla put him on speaker and scrolled around Twitter until she found it.

 Edward N. Passant

@realEdwardNPassant

Me and @KaylaS? Look at her. No way!!!

2:49 PM - 20 Nov 2017

Attached to the tweet was a photograph of Kayla, bent over at an unflattering angle while she picked something off the sidewalk. Morning shadows fell across her shoulders, making it look like she was wearing a burlap sack and a dirty mop over her head.

"Whoa, bad hair day," Kayla said.

"Not why I'm calling." Her editor's usually curt voice was infused with apprehension. "Look at the background."

Kayla suddenly realized where and when the photo had been taken. Outside her apartment building, that very morning. Was a Passant operative stalking her? The shiver of violation ran up her spine.

"You can see the building's address in the photo," her editor said. "Someone's already egged your door. Whatever they do next could be a lot worse. I'm sending a messenger to that school. Give him your apartment key and I'll have movers pack up your things."

"What? You can't seriously—"

"Please don't argue. You stay in that apartment, things could get bad. I won't let myself be responsible for that. The paper will put you up in a hotel until this blows over. We'll take care of it with your landlord."

Kayla hugged herself, breathing hard, fighting tears. A couple of skinny boys in front of the school played rock-paper-scissors for the honor of consoling her.

"Cheer up," her editor said. "This isn't the first time we've dealt with something like this. Now go interview the hell out of that octopus, OK? I'm expecting a Pulitzer for this one."

Kayla tried to laugh, but couldn't.

Thirty-one

Kayla left her key in the school office with instructions to give it to the paper's messenger, then she asked for an escort to the Biology lab.

Piling on to the disappointments of the day, neither Paul Urbina-Pedisich nor Syliva Humphries were there, just a boy who introduced himself as Artie, whose gaze never seemed to get above the level of Kayla's chest.

"Want a shrimp?" He brandished a frozen pink crustacean. "I can heat it up for you."

"No, thanks." She pointed at a big fish tank in the back of the class. "Is that Orville?"

"Yeah. His taxonomy is *O. vulgaris*. Funny name, right? He has a great sense of feel and great vision, and his memory is better than mine. Uh, what was I saying?"

The boy seemed distracted by Kayla walking across the room. Her back was turned but she suspected his gaze had dropped from her chest to her butt. It might have amused her if not for the other events of the day. "You were saying Orville has a good memory," she said.

"Oh, yeah, right. That's why we were able to teach him to communicate with us."

"OK, let's start with that," Kayla said. "Exactly how do you talk with an octopus?"

Artie pulled up a chair for Kayla and then sat down next to her. "Well, if I was another octopus, I'd communicate by changing my shape and color — see?"

Orville seemed to recognize the boy. The octopus flattened itself and went from a light brown to a bluish gray. Artie dumped in a few shrimp and the animal shifted color again, to a pale pink.

"I think that means 'thank you,'" Artie said.

Kayla was starting to think she'd been had. "How do I know you're telling me what the octopus really says? How do I know when you tweet for him, you're not just making it up?"

"Well, for one thing, I don't always agree with Orville's politics. If it were me, for example, I'd probably tweet in favor of free trade."

Kayla had been mostly joking with her editor about this, but she'd been hyping this story to him for months. She didn't want to have to admit she'd been the victim of a prank. "All right, I'll play along," she said. "How does he tell you what to tweet?"

"Mostly we ask him yes or no questions. Like I said before, he has great vision, so Mr. Harrison set up this Morse code thing that lights up inside the tank." He clicked an old-time telegraph transmitter, and a tiny light went on and off inside the tank.

"What did you tell him?" she said.

He looked surprised. "'You're welcome,' of course. No reason to be impolite."

Kayla's impatience mounted. "Let's get down to business, shall we? How does he answer?"

Artie pointed at two levers inside the tank. "Green is yes, and red is no. Watch." He started depressing the transmitter again, translating while he tapped. "Orville, this is Kayla. Can she ask you a question?"

The movements of the octopus were kind of creepy, it just sort of flowed from one place to another. One of its tentacles pressed a lever, and a small green light flashed at one corner of the tank. Artie rewarded Orville with a shrimp.

"Ask away." Artie's expression was one of complete innocence, except when the corners of his mouth quirked up to form a cheeky grin.

"Okay," she drew out the word. "How about this? Do you support Paul Urbina-Pedisich for President of the United States?"

Paul tapped at the transmitter for a bit, the octopus flowed again and the green light repeated itself. Apparently, each answer merited another shrimp.

Kayla pursed her lips. "Do you support Edward N. Passant for President?"

The red light flashed.

She repeated each question. The octopus stayed consistent. Kayla's eyes narrowed almost to slits. "OK, one more. Do you *not* support Edward N. Passant?"

Neither light flashed. The octopus seemed to grow taller, its skin got purplish.

Kayla stared. "What did he say?"

"He said you employed a double-negative." Artie's face flushed. "To be honest, I'm not sure how well he understands English grammar. I mean, he's an octopus."

The door to the lab opened. Paul and Sylvia came in.

"Oh, hi, Kayla," Paul said.

Sylvia's face scrunched up, like if she could've spit acid, there'd have been a hole in the nearest lab table.

Artie bit his lip. He looked around as if searching for a hiding place. Paul stalked right up to him, extended his index finger so that it touched the middle of Artie's chest.

"Your 'pen pal,' it's President Passant, isn't it?"

Artie swallowed but said nothing. Paul said, "You've been telling him things in Pig Latin. Things about me. I promised Sylvia I wouldn't tell you details about LGBTQ meetings, and I didn't. But the first time, I told you I went to it. You told him."

Artie couldn't meet Paul's hot gaze. He couldn't look at Sylvia. He turned around and dumped a handful of shrimp into Orville's tank.

"Yeah, I did it," Artie said, his voice just above a mumble. "So? What of it?"

Thirty-two

Artie's declaration hit Paul like a gut punch. He stood there, barely able to breathe but he was *not* going to cry in front of Kayla. Or Sylvia. He opened his mouth to deliver a poignant yet scathing retort, something so powerful his biographer would include it on the back of a book jacket, so memorable they'd paint it in twelve-foot letters on the wall of his presidential library, but all that came out was, "Really?"

Artie faced him, his face curled into a scowl. "Yeah, really. Why should I care about you, when you obviously don't give a damn about me? We could have run for President together, or at least you could've made me Vice President. But, nooooo, it had to be your new girlfriend, because she's so wonderful. Sylvia, Sylvia, Sylvia, is that all you can ever talk about?"

Behind him, Paul heard a sniffle, then a cough that he was pretty sure belonged to the young woman in question.

"I was so sick of hearing her name that I didn't even care that you stopped talking to me altogether," Artie said.

Paul blinked. "I didn't stop talking to you."

"Yeah? When's the last time that we Skyped?"

"Artie, you live next door."

"When's the last time we played Xbox?"

Artie rubbed his eyes, and Paul couldn't help but do the same. "I've been kind of busy, you know, running for leader of the free world and all."

Soon as he said it, Paul knew it was a mistake.

"Yeah," Artie said. "I've been busy too, sending postcards. Maybe I'll send another one right now."

He ran from the lab, slamming the door behind him. Orville the Octopus squirted a cloud of ink in the tank.

Paul looked at Sylvia, then at Kayla. "I guess this whole thing is kinda my fault. Either way, it's time for me to get over to headquarters and face the music."

"I can drive you," Kayla said. "I don't have anywhere else to go."

Sylvia did her laser-vision, scrunchy face thing again. Paul, as usual, barely noticed.

"Mr. Creed is gonna kill me," he said.

Except Mr. Creed didn't seem to care, one way or the other. He just kept rocking back and forth in his chair, behind his desk, reading polling data or some such.

"Doesn't really matter," he said in his drawling, craggy voice. "Passant's got the homophobic vote locked up, anyway. But there was a chance the gay community wouldn't turn out. They didn't for Alison Denton. No chance of that now, though. They'll walk twenty miles in the snow to pull that lever for you."

"So you're OK with it?" Paul flopped onto the sofa and took a deep breath. There'd been so many ups and downs lately, he might as well have been riding that green-painted see-saw he used to favor in General Wayne Park when he was five.

Mr. Creed chuckled. "We'll put out a statement: 'You don't have to be gay to support gay rights.' Let Passant blather for a couple days about how he's the LGBTQ community's best friend and watch everybody laugh. I call it a net gain."

Kayla stood near the doorway, fiddling with her phone. She handed it to Mr. Creed.

"How about this, you OK with that, too?"

Paul brought up his own Twitter app and scrolled down a little.

His head drooped. "Not again."

 Edward N. Passant

@realEdwardNPassant

If I trafficked in rumors, I'd be talking about @KaylaS and Punky Pablo. What's the age for statutory rape in PA? Terrible!

5:19 PM - 20 Nov 2017

"Because to be totally honest with you," Kayla said. "I'm not OK with it, even a little bit.

Thirty-three

The next morning, Paul woke early. Mr. Creed was coming over at 5:30am to take Paul and Sylvia to Washington for a security briefing, which was apparently offered by the National Security Council to all presidential and vice presidential candidates. The school principal gave them yet another excused absence, making Paul wonder if he could somehow arrange to run for President every year.

The pre-dawn pickup meant he had to wake up a full hour earlier than a standard school day, but that didn't bother Paul on this occasion because it gave him the opportunity to finalize a secret project he'd been working on for weeks, something he could only set up when everyone else in the house was asleep. He put everything in motion, took his shower, grabbed a Pop Tart for breakfast, and walked outside just as the limo pulled up.

Sylvia was already in the backseat, while Mr. Creed sat in the passenger seat next to the Secret Service agent driver. Paul climbed in next to his running mate, who gave him a noncommittal nod but didn't speak. The car pulled away, shrouded in awkward silence, which continued for at least a half hour.

He felt her eyes on him, but when he caught her looking, she didn't turn away like most people would. Just cocked her head to one side and resumed studying his face. Finally, he could take her disconcerting stares no longer.

"It's not true, you know," he said. "About me and Kayla. President Passant made the whole thing up."

Her face pinched in around her nose. "I've seen the way you look at her."

"Well, she's pretty," Paul said. "Guys like me don't get to see many women like her, you know, up close and in person."

"You're not making it any better," she said.

Paul suppressed a shout but couldn't keep his fingers from curling. "Forget it."

"You ought to both forget it," Mr. Creed said from up front. "Classic I-know-you-are-but-what-am-I defense, perfected by third-graders everywhere."

Paul surfed the latest tweets. "Ha! Looks like today I'm not an American."

 Edward N. Passant

@realEdwardNPassant

Extremely credible source says Punky Pablo's mom an illegal immigrant from *Mexico*. Is PP even a US citizen? Make him produce his birth certificate!

3:03 AM - 21 Nov 2017

Mr. Creed's voice sounded like he was contemplating a nap. "Passant is one of those people who, if something works for them once, they keep going back to it, like a middle-aged man who still tries to peek into women's locker rooms like he did when he was fifteen."

Sylvia gave Paul the eye.

"Don't look at me." He held up both hands. "I've never done that."

"We'll issue a statement that you'll produce your birth certificate the day after he produces his tax returns, and be done with it," Mr. Creed said. A few moments later his head nodded off toward the door.

They got snagged in some Beltway traffic, but pulled up to an office building near the Capitol three minutes before their 9am appointment. Mr. Creed roused himself and led them inside. Near the elevators, a Senator waved at them. Paul recognized him but unfortunately Delaware wasn't wearing his name tag so Paul had to avoid introductions.

"Hey, Mr. President. Well, soon anyway, right?" The guy shook everybody's hand, including a maintenance worker who just happened to walk by. "I heard the rumors about you and that attractive reporter." He gave Paul's shoulder a playful punch. "Nice work." Paul tried to wave him off while Sylvia's face slowly turned maroon, but Delaware didn't take the hint. "Smart play, too. You should paste pictures of that woman everywhere. Would definitely help you with white males. Well, gotta go."

Paul jumped into the elevator before he could be accosted by anybody else he knew. Mr. Creed led them to an office door and knocked. Almost immediately the door was yanked open by a pear-shaped man with thinning hair, thick-lensed eyeglasses, and an untucked shirt.

The man blinked. "You're here!" He stumbled out and gave them all big hugs. "I'm so happy you've come."

Paul looked to Mr. Creed, who shrugged. The man led them inside. He smelled like Paul's grandmother who lived alone with fourteen cats. "My name is Joe and I'll be your NSC briefer for the duration of the campaign. I was President Passant's briefer, too, from the moment he was elected last year until the day he resigned."

"Wow," Sylvia said. "If you did briefings all that time, you must be really good at it."

Joe's shoulders drooped. He slumped into a chair. "President Passant didn't always show up for our scheduled briefings."

"That's OK. I'm sure you still did a whole bunch, right?"

"This will be my first," Joe said. "But I've had tons of practice, by myself, in the mirror." He looked around. "Can I get you something to eat? I baked chocolate chip cookies."

They assured him they were fine. "OK," he said. "Where should we start? Japan? They used to be our friends but now they hate us. Germany? France? They both used to be our friends but now they hate us, too. China? Nah, they always hated us. How about Russia? They keep sending us gifts but they all have surveillance chips hidden inside."

He looked up at his guests. "Oh dear, did I say that out loud? You spend so much time by yourself, you develop all kinds of bad habits."

Mr. Creed smiled. "How about the Middle East, Joe? A classic, right? Can't go wrong with that."

Joe beamed at him. Mr. Creed got up to leave. "Have fun, kids. I'll be back for you in a few hours."

Joe the Briefer clapped his hands together. He gave them briefing books and projected six-color maps onto the wall and wrote a bunch of stuff on a chalk board. He nearly swooned when Paul took out a three-ring binder and began to take notes.

It was very comprehensive, and very long, though they didn't get a whole lot of information they hadn't already learned in 9th grade Social Studies. Paul breathed a sigh when Mr. Creed returned.

"So soon?" Joe said. "Well, that was so much fun. Promise me you'll come back, OK? Next time, maybe we can do the Americas. Do you like pie? I know a place where I can get a really nice pie. Or cake, if you like that better. What's your favorite soda?"

They got up and put on their coats. Joe's eyes seemed a little moist. "Maybe you can stay just a little longer?" He grabbed Paul's sleeve. "Come on, don't leave now. Just a few more minutes?"

Mr. Creed extricated Paul's arm and led them away. They could hear Joe the Briefer's wails all the way down the hall.

"No, no! Don't leave me alone again. Please!

They escaped the building and Paul checked Twitter again.

 Edward N. Passant

@realEdwardNPassant

Happy Channukah, Paul Pedisich!

1:14 PM - 21 Nov 2017

Sylvia frowned. "Is Pedisich even a Jewish name?"

"Think the deplorables know the difference?" Mr. Creed said. "Looks like they're in full spaghetti mode over at Passant headquarters. Throw it at the wall and see what sticks."

"Should I tweet back?" Paul said.

Mr. Creed patted Paul on the shoulder. "Wouldn't do you any good, son. I know it's hard, but you're just going to have to sit back and act like the grown up in this campaign. Lord knows somebody has to."

"OK, I'll try," Paul said. "But is any of this going to hurt us?"

Mr. Creed shrugged. "Past forty-eight hours we've pulled in the LGBTQ vote, the Latino vote, and the Jewish vote. Pretty good couple of days in my book."

He called for the car and they waited by the curb. "Hopefully soon, he'll call you black and Asian, and we can pull a clean sweep."

Thirty-four

"Nothing's working." President Passant stomped on the floor like a petulant kindergartner. "We're not getting any traction."

"That's not entirely true, Mr. President," Stanton said. Much as he found Stew Cannon's tactics distasteful, he had to admit they were often effective. "We've successfully changed the subject. At least nobody's talking about you groping that female reporter any more."

"You think it's time to bring out the big guns?" Stew hammered away at his laptop's keyboard. "I've got one thermonuclear bomb in stock, but once we use it, we're done. You sure you want to deploy it now?"

The talk of "big guns" and "thermonuclear bombs" made Stanton just a tad nervous. After the smoke cleared, it was always he who had to put on the hazmat suit and clear away the rubble. He was about to ask Stew for details when President Passant spoke first.

"Do it," he said. "And in case it doesn't work, I'm going to make a phone call. Fix this problem once and for all."

President Passant stalked away. Stanton decided he didn't want to know.

*   *   *

Paul drowsed off practically the minute the car pulled off the curb. By the time Sylvia shook him awake, they were stuck in rush hour traffic, about ten miles south of Philadelphia. The lowering sun stabbed into him from the side window.

"What?" Paul tried to focus his eyes but between the sun and his sleepiness, everything was one big blur.

"Is he awake?" Mr. Creed's voice had lost its usual folksy charm.

"What?" Paul said again.

His campaign manager shoved a phone into his hand, but Paul shook his head, unable to focus on it. Mr. Creed snarled.

"Justin Bieber? Seriously? *That's* what you listen to? You couldn't have told us that when we vetted you?"

"What are you talking about?" Paul said. "I don't listen to Justin Bieber."

"Well, it's all over the internet that you do." Mr. Creed snatched back the phone and dialed. "What a disaster. We're going to need serious damage control for this one. Look at that, our polls are already starting to tank."

He held his fingers a half-inch apart. "To think I was *this* close to a pretty good couple of days."

The car dropped Paul off in front of his house. Mr. Creed said, "I'll call you in a few to tell you where we are on this. Get a good night's sleep, son, you're going to need it."

The front door had barely shut behind him when his mother called from upstairs. "Paul Urbina-Pedisich, get up here *right now!*"

He raced up the stairs. His Mom pointed toward a door-sized piece of plywood leaning against the wall, covered in realistic-looking brick-face wallpaper, then at a piece of yellowed parchment, affixed to the wallpaper by a glop of red, antique wax, and containing a quote from the *Cask of Amontillado*.

"Your father and I were awakened this morning by your brother trying to headbutt his way through the 'brick wall' blocking his doorway and secured by those five sturdy two-by-fours," she said. "His cell phone was on the floor of the hall bathroom, the landline next to his bed was disconnected, the circuit breaker for his room was turned off, and that note was written in *your* handwriting. What do you have to say for yourself, young man?"

"Ooh, can I see what it looks like from the inside?" Paul blinked. "I mean, I've never seen any of this before in my life."

"You don't straighten out, young man, you'll find out what *real* bricks look like from the inside. Do you understand me?"

"But Mom, last week you should've seen what he—"

"I don't care what he did last week. You're the older brother, start acting like it."

The small, evil one hunched around the corner, fixing Paul with a ghoulish grin.

"It's not fair," Paul said. "You never care what he does to me."

His cell phone rang, the caller ID said it was Mr. Creed. Before Paul could answer, his mother plucked the phone from his hand and put it to her ear.

"Yes?" She listened for a couple seconds.

"No, you can't talk to him." Her face hardened. "Because the Democratic nominee for President of the United States is *grounded*."

Thirty-five

Heath Dunbar bowed his head while his fiancé's grandfather said grace before the Thanksgiving feast. It was Heath's first holiday dinner with his fiancé's family since they'd become engaged. Her hand felt so warm, clasped in his own, but she only had eyes for her grandpa, who had founded the LCPVM and thus had had the authority not only to bestow upon himself the rank of General, but also — largely because he commanded lots of people with guns — to insist that everyone he knew address him as such. Long past the age where he could physically engage in LCPVM exercises, the General nonetheless retained his command, because you're never too old to boss other people around.

"I spoke yesterday to Brigadier Haig, from the Commonwealth office," the General said. "You'll never guess who called him the other day."

Heath opened his mouth but the General cut him off with a curt gesture. "I said, 'You'll never guess.' The call came from none other than President Edward N. Passant, himself. Far as I'm concerned, still our one and only Commander in Chief."

The old man went on for the next 20 minutes, about the "travesty" of President Passant's treatment at the hands of the dishonest press and the liberal elite, about the need for constant vigilance, about the willingness to defend themselves against the "infestation" of their beloved country by terrorists and "inferior" races and, above all, for someone to pass him the white meat and mashed potatoes. Everyone at the table knew better than to interrupt, watching him instead with rapt attention, some more genuine than others. The adoring mindlessness of his fiancé's expression gave Heath a little shiver. He didn't know any Muslims, but he knew two black men, one Asian woman, and had once actually met someone whose grandmother was Mexican, and *none* of them had seemed inferior to him.

Eventually, the General got to the point. "And so, the President of the United States has invited us, the members of the Lycoming County Pennsylvania Volunteer Militia, to a dinner in his honor, exactly one week from today, in the cradle of our country's liberty, Philadelphia, Pennsylvania."

He looked around the table. "We will all be attending."

*   *   *

Paul's grounding corresponded with the Thanksgiving holiday, all the way through the end of the weekend. He'd gone to school for the half day on Wednesday, but had to go straight home after and sit in his room reading about the Emoluments Clause instead of going to his friends' Xbox tournament, which he actually didn't mind so much because the tournament was at Artie's and he wasn't sure he really wanted to be in the same room as his former best friend.

Thanksgiving dinner was the largest Paul could ever remember. They had to set up a long, rented table in the living room because the dining room table wouldn't fit everyone. Naturally, the two Secret Service guys, whose job was to shadow Paul's every step rather than haunt their own families, had to be included. Mr. Creed had invited himself, refusing to be denied access to his candidate for five full days. Paul's Dad had suggested inviting Sylvia and her parents, with whom he'd bonded over the misfortune of having kids who ran for national office instead of more usual teenage pursuits like underage drinking and making out in the backseats of their parents' Toyotas. They probably would have invited Orville the Octopus too, except the cephalopod was too busy basking in the glory of reaching 300,000 Twitter followers, in the wake of his big interview. Plus, he only ate shrimp. Finally, when Paul's Mom had heard about Kayla being forced to give up her apartment, she had insisted on her coming as well, something Sylvia chose to take out on Paul.

If he wasn't within a few feet of his running mate, she made laser-eyes at him until he trudged over to present himself. If he *was* within speaking distance, she made a show of getting up and flouncing away to the furthest corner of the room. At least Paul was getting his exercise.

Paul's Dad did the cooking, which was great if you enjoyed well-prepared, spicy, exotic cuisine. Less great if all you wanted was meat and potatoes. Paul picked at his meal, re-arranging the food on his plate so it looked like he ate something.

"This turkey *satay* is outrageous," Sylvia's Mom said. "And you have to give me the recipe for the yam curry. I insist."

"Sure," his Dad said. "The key is grinding the *Chaat masala* yourself."

Paul's brother sat hunched over, mumbling and doing something with his hands under the table. His Vodou ritual magic rarely worked, but to be on the safe side, Paul elected not to eat or drink anything that had passed his brother's side of the table. He tried to warn Sylvia, Kayla, and Mr. Creed with sign language, but he wasn't sure if his message got through.

Mr. Creed raised his wine glass. "Less than two weeks to go," he said. "The final stretch begins after the bipartisan dinner, featuring both candidates, exactly one week from tomorrow."

"What kind of dinner?" Paul's Mom said.

"Sort of like the Al Smith dinner where both candidates speak and recite a few one-liners, except this one's here in Philadelphia. If we're lucky, Passant will be as off-key as he was last year. Either way, I think we ought to play nice. We'll work up some jokes this week."

Dessert got a little awkward. Mr. Creed kept talking about their falling poll numbers and hinting that another three days of candidate radio silence might irreparably damage the campaign. Paul's Mom kept talking about the importance of discipline and hinting that Mr. Creed wouldn't make much of a parent.

Kayla didn't say much, but she feverishly took notes whenever she thought nobody was looking.

Paul was almost glad when the meal was over so he could be exiled to his room again.

Thirty-six

On his way to the bathroom that night, Paul snuck into his parents' room to check his phone, which they'd stowed in the same exact hiding spot as every confiscated item since his favorite Power Ranger action figure when he was six.

After one look at his Twitter feed, he wished they'd found a different spot this time. President Passant had taken full advantage of his opponent's absence, shooting tweet after tweet into the webosphere. Bam, boom, bing.

 Edward N. Passant

@realEdwardNPassant

Where's Punky Pablo? Taking a nap after milk and cookies?

3:41 PM - 22 Nov 2017

Edward N. Passant

@realEdwardNPassant

Who listens to Justin Bieber? Frilly little girls in pink dresses & Punky Pablo. Which would you want defending US from terrorists? Toss up!

3:42 PM - 22 Nov 2017

 Edward N. Passant

@realEdwardNPassant

Every poll has me winning big! Adios, Punky Pablo!

3:43 PM - 22 Nov 2017

Paul tweeted nothing in return, both because Mr. Creed had warned him against doing so and because he didn't want to get into deeper trouble with his mother, who was a crackerjack at reading a date-stamp.

Instead he surveyed the news sites. In a CNN interview, Mr. Creed pointed out that, though the polls were tightening considerably, the only one in which President Passant was actually leading was an instant poll of his immediate relatives. Most of Mr. Creed's efforts, however, had gone toward inciting op-eds demanding President Passant release his tax returns.

President Passant repeated his promise to release the returns once the IRS had completed its audit, until the "dishonest media" reminded him the audit had finished six months earlier. Paul didn't see his opponent's next response until his Mom returned his phone for keeps Sunday morning.

 Edward N. Passant

@realEdwardNPassant

Forget about disclosure. I have it on very good authority that Punky Pablo has never even *filed* a tax return. What's he hiding?

4:58 AM - 25 Nov 2017

The moment Paul's hand touched the phone, it rang. A reporter whose rapidly announced name sounded like every other reporter's rapidly-announced name heard over a crackly, three-bar cell phone connection.

"I keep telling everyone, I *don't* listen to Justin Bieber," Paul said.

"Sure you don't," the reporter said. "What do you say about your falling poll numbers? Better, what about your tax returns? President Passant says he'll release his if you do the same. What do you say to that?"

"Release my tax returns? Is he brain-damaged? I'm fifteen years old. Other than shoveling my neighbor's driveway three times a year, my income is my allowance. I've never filed a tax return in my life."

"Awesome quote." The reporter sounded like he was shoulder-dancing. "Thanks, you've made my month."

Paul ended the call and flopped onto his bed. He had no idea what he'd done wrong, but he was pretty sure Mr. Creed wouldn't be happy.

He spent the rest of the day dodging the exact same three questions. By 9pm he was exhausted, both physically and emotionally. If he spoke to one more reporter, he was fairly certain he'd lose it. He said goodnight to his parents without them even asking, brushed his teeth, and climbed under his covers.

Sleep didn't come. His frustration and anger ate at him until the whole room seemed to be tinged in red. One hour, two hours, two and a half. Finally, he snatched up his phone. Nothing else had worked, maybe surfing Twitter one last time would calm his nerves.

Not really, no. He barely refrained from impaling the phone on his souvenir version of the Washington Monument. Did President Passant never sleep? His latest tweet included a thumbnail photo of a piece of Paul's homework from a couple months before.

 Edward N. Passant

@realEdwardNPassant

High school lets Punky Pablo write his papers in *Spanish*. Somebody tell them this is America. Sad! *#EnglishOnly #TakeBackOurSchools*

11:52 PM - 26 Nov 2017

"That's it! I can't take it anymore." Paul pounded out a tweet and hit send without further reflection. It was either that or smash all his furniture into little bits.

 Paul U-P

@meltingPUP

It was a paper for Spanish class, doofus!

11:53 PM - 26 Nov 2017

Calm washed through him. He tossed the phone onto his night table and rolled onto his side, pulling the covers up to his neck.

"At least I put *that* problem to bed," he said as he drifted off.

Thirty-seven

The next day, Mr. Creed requested the pleasure of Paul's presence during lunch-and-learn. Paul got the usual stares as he wended through the halls to meet the car out front of the school, although maybe more so. Even the jocks steered clear of him.

"Ooh, wouldn't want to get on your bad side, would we?"

Rather than the usual place in Center City, the Secret Service drove him back to his own house, where Mr. Creed waited in the den, watching a segment on CNN. He hit the pause button when Paul walked into the room.

"Did you tell a reporter you've never filed a tax return in your life?" Mr. Creed said.

Paul eyed the exit, but there was no way out of this one.

"Maybe," he said in a small, cagey voice.

Mr. Creed said nothing, just pressed play and returned his attention to the TV.

"I don't care how small the payments are," a panelist said. "I don't care if he blows it off as a periodic shoveling gig or a weekly stipend. Whatever you call it, it's unreported income. Do

164

we really want the President of the United States involved in something like that? I say—"

Another panelist interrupted. "I think we're going to have to live with the fact that *neither* candidate appears forthcoming about their finances. It's just a fact of life in today's politics."

The host cut her off, too. "You're watching Henderson Hooper 180, and we'll get to all that in a bit. But first, let's start with the pressing question on everybody's mind right now: is Edward N. Passant a doofus?"

Mr. Creed turned off the television. "So, now *you're* the name-calling bully. Someone is also quoting you as describing Passant as 'brain-damaged.'" He shrugged. "That one, I'm probably OK with. What worries me more is this."

He handed Paul his phone, which showed a tweet with a picture of Paul's brother looking like he'd just lost a prizefight.

Paul bit his lip. He looked closely at the photo. "That's bogus. It has to be photoshopped."

"Oh?"

"Absolutely. The shiner was on his *left* eye."

Mr. Creed's face creased further that it already was. "That doesn't make me feel a whole lot better."

"It wasn't my fault," Paul said in a whiny voice. "He did it to himself, banging his head against the Cask of Amontillado."

"I have no idea what that means, and I don't want to. What I want is to know how much more of this behavior is going to come out?"

Paul flailed his fists in the air. "It's not *fair*. I didn't *do* anything."

"Tell that to the American people." Mr. Creed slid some papers across the coffee table. "Internal poll, conducted this morning. 'Which presidential candidate do you consider a bully?' See those boxes there at the bottom? Edward Passant, fifty-two percent, Paul Urbina-Pedisich, forty-six percent. That's almost within the margin of error. A week ago, that spread was seventy-five points."

He rocked back and forth in his chair, then his gaze sharpened beneath his wrinkled brow. "A politician, a priest, and a clown walk into a bar. The bartender says, 'Is this a joke?' The clown says, 'No, we're the new Administration.'" The old man rocked some more. "I've told that little ditty at political dinners for six administrations worth of Presidents, and it gets the same laughs every time. Do you know why?"

Paul shook his head. He knew Mr. Creed was blaming him for something, he just didn't know what, yet.

"Because, to the vast majority of Americans, every administration is the same. They're pro-life or pro-choice, pro-tax or anti-tax, and if no candidate differentiates himself then the people just vote party line and the winner depends on who can get the biggest turnout.

"Last election, the Democrats ran a woman who had lived in the White House for eight years, was a United States Senator for eight years, and Secretary of State for five years. If you count her time as a lawyer, she served in all three branches of government. She was without doubt the best-credentialed person ever to run for President of the United States."

His breath rattled in his lungs. "And then a flimflam salesman who'd never even been elected to his local Chamber of Commerce convinced a significant portion of the public that the two of them were the same. People started saying, 'I don't like either one of them.' The Democrats who stayed home, the moderate Republicans who pulled the Passant lever. He dragged her down to his level, created a false equivalence.

"I didn't think that was possible with you. You're an innocent, no past, no skeletons, nothing for him to dig his claws into. But it's happening, he's doing it again, and you're his prime accomplice. You're helping him. This is *your* doing."

He stopped rocking, leaned forward, and fixed his sharp gaze on Paul. "So tell me, Mr. Nominee. What are you going to do to fix it?"

Paul blinked back tears. It wasn't fair. He smacked his fist into his thigh. He hadn't done anything. "I have to go back to school now," he said.

Running for President wasn't so much fun anymore.

Thirty-eight

Paul sat in the circle at the LGBTQ meeting, half-listening to someone detailing a homophobic taunt they'd heard at the mall. He tried to catch Sylvia's eye, but she once again sat as far from him as possible and refused to even look at him.

"Who's next?" the leader said.

John 86 stood up, today wearing a green dress that somehow made him look demure, in a Godzilla kind of way. "I hurt somebody again," he said. "Last week at the game. I could have tackled him more gently — he was a little guy, he would've gone down — but I don't know what comes over me. I just live for the big hits."

The other John patted his teammate on the shoulder. "I know exactly how you feel. I agree we should try to reduce violence in the world, but I can't help it. I guess I like it."

The group discussed ways to reduce domestic violence and the seeking of a healthy balance between the brutality of war and the SportsCenter top ten. The leader checked the time. "Anybody else?"

Paul raised his hand.

"Paul?" the leader said. "What a nice surprise. I don't think you've ever spoken at one of our meetings before."

"It's not about LGBTQ issues," he said.

"That's OK."

Paul took a deep breath then started unloading. After the first word, it seemed like he couldn't stop. He talked about the pressure, the unfairness, the loneliness, and finally the betrayal at the hands of his best friend.

"I'm sure it was Artie who gave President Passant the Spanish paper and the photoshopped picture of my brother, but I can't believe it. I feel like I want to take a baseball bat to the back of his head."

"Probably not the best play if you want to get out from under your new bully image," John 69 said. "Trust me, I know."

Paul watched Sylvia out of the corner of his eye. She didn't say anything, but at least she looked at him. That is, until he tried facing her directly, at which time she quickly turned to the person of indeterminate gender on her right.

The meeting ended. Paul wasn't sure if he felt better or not. He trudged out after everybody else, not particularly paying attention to anybody or anything.

Someone grabbed his shoulder from behind.

Paul turned and blinked. John 86 towered over him. "Can I give you a nickel of free advice?" he said.

"Uh, OK," Paul said. "About what?"

John 86 tilted his chin toward the receding form of Sylvia, who for once wasn't skipping, seeming instead to slog under the weight of her backpack.

Paul felt his face pinch in. "What about her?"

John shook his head. "Nothing about her. I'm talking about you. If you think being President of the United States is more important than the love of a good partner, you're a lot stupider than I thought."

Without another word, he turned and headed toward the boy's room down the hall, his green dress swishing as he walked.

*   *   *

"It's Tuesday, November twenty-eighth, the election is one week from today," Kayla said to Lincoln Echols Creed. "How are you feeling about it?"

She sat with Creed in his office, waiting for the Democratic candidates to get out of school. The man looked five years older than he had when they'd met two months before.

"I'd feel better if any of these polls accurately reflected the youth vote. The sampling models we've employed in the past are useless this time." He pointed at a map on the wall with way too many red states. "At least I hope they're useless. If the eighteen-to-twenty-nine crowd turns out at its traditional rate, we're cooked."

Paul and Sylvia appeared in the doorway, standing as far away from each other as possible in the small foyer outside the office.

"We got trouble, son," Creed said. "The public thinks both candidates are bullying, petulant, children, which means they'll probably vote for the older one."

"Thank you for that. I'm very appreciative," Paul said in that faux-bland, passively sarcastic voice boys seem to master overnight on their 14th birthday.

"The people think you and Passant are both equally likely to hurt an innocent or lose control of your temper at an inopportune moment."

"He tried to have me *killed*," Paul said. "Doesn't that count for anything?"

"That was almost three months ago, son. Ancient history. Once it's out of the news cycle, can't expect the public to remember it even happened. But forget about that, that's not what's going to sink us. No, if we want to win, we need to energize the youth vote, especially young males, who never turn out. 'The Edward' did a pretty good job depressing that demo with the Justin Bieber thing."

"For the seventy-fifth time, I do *not* listen to Justin Bieber."

"Preachin' to the choir, kid."

Paul whipped his phone from his pocket. He tapped away with both thumbs.

"What are you doing?" Creed's eyes narrowed.

"Stabilizing my poll numbers," Paul said. He finished what he was typing and held it out for the others to see.

 Paul U-P

@meltingPUP

You see the game last night? Boy, those refs SUCK!!!

3:57 PM - 28 Nov 2017

"What game you talking about?"

"Does it matter?"

Creed's body shook with silent laughter. He winked at Kayla. "Kid's got more game than I thought."

Thirty-nine

Heath had to take an extra day off from the bottling plant to make the trip to the big city to meet President Passant in person. He and his fiancé received the honor of riding with the Colonel, mostly because the General said so. The SUV rode low to the ground, in part due to Heath's fiancé packing all their handguns and shotguns, her favorite AK-47, the Barrett M82 she'd bought online, and the old AR-15 her daddy gave her as a birthday present the day she turned nine. Heath thought maybe they might not need all that firepower for a rubber chicken dinner in a ritzy hotel.

The Colonel came down on Heath's fiancé's side "Bring every automatic and semi-automatic you got," he said. "Weapons that weasel-faced little spic jew will steal from us if we don't come through in this election."

"Do we really need those sorts of weapons to go hunting or protect our homes?" Heath asked, once he'd ascertained the SUV didn't contain a latrine. "You wouldn't say the Second Amendment affords us the right to keep chemical weapons or nuclear bombs, would you?"

"Of course not! Don't be ridiculous," the Colonel scoffed loudly. But at the first rest stop he cornered Heath by the Slim Jims and whispered, "You know where we can get some?"

Heath stayed quiet the rest of the trip.

*   *   *

Kayla peeked her head inside the small office where Sylvia was reading. She watched the youngster for a bit, the way she nibbled on the ends of her hair while she studied, the way her feet twitched absently, the way she seemed to hum to herself without sound.

Sylvia looked up. She gave a startled shiver. "Oh, hi. I didn't see you. Paul's not here. I don't know where he went."

"That's OK," Kayla said. "I came to talk to you."

"Me? Why?" The girl half-turned away. Her voice was a bit higher than usual.

"Just to see how you're doing. Everyone's focusing on Paul, but this has to be stressful for you, too."

"You have no idea," Sylvia said. "I'm supposed to give a talk to a women's group this evening. What do I know about their issues?"

"Don't sell yourself short. I'm sure you know plenty. They don't want to be treated like helpless little girls, either. Remember that."

Sylvia tilted her head to one side, so that her hair lay flat on one cheek, then she tilted the other way. "You know, my whole life I always wanted to be treated like a grown-up. But now that most people do treat me that way, I don't think I like it."

Kayla laughed. "I'm not sure I always like it, either. All that responsibility. But I guess you get used to it."

She came into the room and put her arm around Sylvia's shoulder. "You don't have anything to worry about from me, you know."

"What?" Sylvia half-turned away again. "I don't know what you mean?"

"I'm almost twice as old as he is. And even if I wasn't, that's not why I'm here. I'm not a threat to the two of you being together."

A slow blush climbed from Sylvia's neck to her cheeks. "I guess I haven't been so nice to you, have I?"

Kayla shrugged. "I hadn't noticed."

She gave Sylvia's hand a squeeze as she left.

*   *   *

Seamus packed his things, not that he had many. Or needed many, this was tonight only. He'd probably be gone before they cleared the fish course at the bipartisan dinner tomorrow. Either that, or dead.

He'd been studying his adversary, watching the ebb and flow of the campaign, mapping locations, monitoring phone calls. The best opportunity would come tomorrow, late Friday afternoon or early evening, at or around the dinner.

He intended to be there.

He tossed two phones into his bag, both fully charged and loaded with his music. Not Gordon Lightfoot, something better this time. Or worse, depending on how you looked at it. He glanced at his watch.

Time to go. He needed an extra hour to shake the CIA tail he assumed was out there. He slung his bag over his shoulder and headed for the train station.

It would all be over in 24 hours.

Forty

Paul found Artie in the Bio lab, attempting to come up with yet another subject for Orville the Octopus to tweet about. Pretty much all Artie did any more, from what Paul heard. Between Kayla's interview — which had been picked up by almost every media outlet in the country — and the series of hostile Passant tweets ending with, "I eat octopus for breakfast," Orville had been adding followers like crazy. Eight million by last count, not quite up to President Passant's 37 million, but gaining.

Artie looked up, then turned back to the telegraph transmitter. "Oh, it's you."

"It is," Paul said. "And it was you who sent my Spanish paper and the picture of my brother to President Passant." A statement, not a question.

"What do you care?" Artie continued relaying his message to the octopus.

Paul let out a wild howl. He ran up to Artie, grabbed him by the shoulder, spun him around. He reared back a fist but almost immediately dropped it.

"What do I *care*? About you sabotaging my presidential campaign, about you taking a picture after my brother injured himself and telling people *I* did it? Are you deranged?"

"Hey, that's a lie," Artie said. "I never told anyone you did it. I sent Passant the Spanish paper ages ago. And I sent your brother's pic the last time you yelled at me, the day before the Cask of Amontillado, way before the bully stuff. I thought it'd be funny to photoshop the black eye. I was going to do horns and cloven hooves, too, but I got bored."

He gave a classic so-there look, picked up his phone and began typing his tweet. He tapped a pen against his chin. "How do you spell 'megalomaniac'?"

Paul folded his arms and waited. After a minute or so, he started bouncing his foot on the rubber floor tiles.

"Cut it out. I'm working," Artie said.

Paul kept it up. "That all you got?" he said.

"All right, look." Artie jumped off his lab stool and paced around the room. "I'm sorry, OK? But I got so angry." His voice got louder and louder. "Why'd they pick *you* to run for President, and not me? Nobody's even asked me to run for president of the robotics club. What have you ever done, other than tweet badly and accidentally blow up the chemistry lab that one time? What makes you better than me, huh?"

Paul dropped his arms and sighed. "I don't know, Artie. Probably nothing. But I'll tell you this much, I'd never in a million years sell out my best friend over something as lame as being President of the United States."

Artie tried to keep up his scowl, but the corners of his mouth quirked upward. "You kidding? You almost sold me out over a Pokémon card when we were eight."

Paul smiled for the first time in days. "My point, exactly. *That* was important."

176

Artie's shoulders slumped. "I really am sorry. I don't know what came over me. Maybe it's this octopus thing. Eight million followers? That's a ton of pressure on me to deliver, and it never stops. It's like a full-time job."

"Tell me about it," Paul said.

"Yeah, I guess you got it even worse, don't you? I don't envy you, pal. I mean, I *do* envy you, but I don't... well, you know."

"Yeah, I do," Paul said. "Listen, I gotta go practice my jokes for tomorrow's dinner. See you Saturday? Maybe I can come over and kick your ass on Xbox."

"No way, dude. You won't come close."

Paul felt lighter as he climbed into the Secret Service car, even though he still kinda wanted to bean Artie with a baseball bat. He hadn't thought it would, but his friend's apology really helped, made him feel like all his other worries weren't insurmountable, either.

Apologies meant something.

He groaned. He knew what he had to do.

The Secret Service guy glanced at him via the rear-view mirror. "You OK, sir?"

"I'm fine," Paul said. "And you don't have to call me sir. I'm fifteen years old. You probably have a kid my age."

"Three years older, actually. She'll be voting in her first election next week."

Paul wondered if she'd be voting for him, or whether he was even worth voting for. Soon as they got to headquarters he went looking for Sylvia.

He found her shrugging her arms into her coat sleeves. "I have to go," she said. "I'm speaking at a women's group tonight to tell them nobody has the right to treat them like little girls or tell them what to do with their own bodies. As if they didn't already know that."

"I just need a minute," Paul said.

She flopped down in her chair and folded her arms in front of her chest. "Yes, sir, Mr. President? How may I serve you?"

"That's not what I meant."

He found another chair and pulled it close to Sylvia. She seemed to consider pulling away, but didn't.

"I apologize, OK?" he said. "I was a jerk to you and I was wrong and I'll try not to do it anymore. I think you're great. There's a reason everybody likes you, including me. I think you'd make the best Vice President ever. Way better than I'd do as President. Not that any of that matters, at this point."

He stood up. "So, I'm sorry. I realize you probably still hate me, and if you do, that's OK, I deserve it. But I wanted to tell you."

He turned to leave but found himself falling back into his chair. Sylvia threw her arms around him and buried her face in his neck, dragging him down with a tackle that would have done John 86 proud.

She snuffled but didn't let go of him, mumbled something that sounded like, "I'm sorry too." She let go slowly, stood up and wiped her eyes and cheeks.

Then she punched him, hard, on the arm.

"Don't ever do it again," she said.

Forty-one

It was the best dinner Heath ever had. Not rubber chicken at all, a big, thick steak. And beer in a frosty mug, and soup with ham, and a salad with tiny cranberries in it, and little sherbets between courses, and all the potatoes-with-cheese-on-top that he could eat. The only thing he wasn't crazy about was the vegetable.

"Yech, I hate broccoli," he said.

"Dunbar!" the Colonel said, looking around for any skulking members of the press. "We do *not* tolerate 'hate speech' in the LCPVM." He leaned in and spoke softly. "Though I think we ought to switch to another table. Our waiter looks like he might be one of them Muslims."

Heath wondered how you could tell someone's religion just by looking at him but decided it best not to ask. Instead he said, "Is it strange that we're the only people here? The LCPVM, I mean. There aren't even any reporters or other politicians or anybody."

"President wants to congratulate us for our vigilance and patriotism," the Colonel said. "Nothing strange about that."

179

"Except wouldn't he want to congratulate other militia groups too?" There must have been a whole bunch of vigilant and patriotic brigades out there, maybe even some that didn't spend the majority of their time watching television at the Stars-and-Stripes Tavern.

"You ask too many questions, Dunbar. Someday that's going to get you into trouble."

The chords of the *Battle Hymn of the Republic* blared over the sound system. A moment after the recorded chorus sang, "...His truth is marching on," President Passant strode onto the temporary stage at the back of the room. Heath had to turn his chair to see him, though he kept one eye on the table in case the Muslim waiter brought dessert.

"We're having a lot of fun," President Passant said. "In five days, we're going to win another election. Every poll has me in the lead, every single one. Have you seen Punky Pablo recently? I know I haven't, I guess maybe his nap schedule interferes with his campaign. I've been told he still wears diapers, can you believe it? I don't know if that's true, but that's what people are saying. That would be really crazy, wouldn't it? Really crazy. Can you imagine having to have his diaper changed in the middle of negotiating with the Chinese? I can't."

The Colonel nodded at everything President Passant said. Heath's fiancé nodded too. Everyone at the table nodded, except Heath, who was still watching for the chocolate mousse. They all cheered at every pause, even if the pause came in the middle of a word.

The President beamed over the entire LCPVM. "Our movement is about taking the government back. For you, the people. It's about America first. It's about keeping our country safe from Radical. Islamic. Terrorism."

Heath surreptitiously glanced at the waiter, but the man didn't even grimace, he just went about his job. Maybe he wasn't a Muslim after all, or maybe he still was, but wasn't a terrorist? How would that fit into the President's worldview?

"I don't have to tell you about myself. You all know," President Passant said. "And you know it without hearing from the most dishonest group of people in the world — the lying media."

Heath's fiancé booed. The Colonel hissed. The President went on. "Well, here's what the biased media won't tell you: they don't believe in the Second Amendment, they're in favor of strict gun control. No, more than that, they want to take every one of your guns away. That's why they're helping Punky Pablo. He doesn't believe in the Second Amendment, either. He's a threat to your liberty, your freedom, to your very way of *life*." He held both hands up in the air, palms forward. "We all know who he'll pick for judges. But you've seen who I pick. I've put more pro-gun justices on the Supreme Court than any President in history, that's a fact. Most ever."

Heath said, "I don't see how that's possible. He only appointed one justice."

"Shush!" his fiancé said.

The President straightened at the podium. He spoke even louder than before. "It would be a horrible day if Punky Pablo wins on Tuesday and appoints anti-gun judges. Horrible. And once that happens, your guns are as good as gone. There's nothing you can do, folks. Nothing."

The mood in the room got darker. The Colonel grumbled under his breath.

"Although for you Second Amendment people, maybe there is, I don't know," President Passant said.

The Colonel surged to his feet. "You bet there is!"

Everyone stomped their feet and shouted their agreement.

"Yeah, maybe there is," the President said. "Maybe even tomorrow afternoon, before the bipartisan dinner, when Pablo is scheduled to be driven by Secret Service agents from his school to the venue at exactly four-thirty pm. Like I say, maybe. I don't know."

He nodded to himself, gave the crowd two thumbs up. "It's been great talking to you. Remember to vote on Tuesday, and together we'll make America safe for gun owners again."

He walked off to thunderous applause. Heath wondered if dessert was ever coming.

*   *   *

Stanton paced back and forth in the antechamber between the dining area and the hotel kitchen. He'd felt adrift ever since President Passant's latest firing spree, which lowered the axe on 16 staffers including Stanton's yoga instructor. He felt adrift now, tired, off-center.

The dining room burst into ovation. President Passant swaggered past, into an unoccupied ballroom. He sat and rubbed his hands together, wearing a smug grin.

Stanton followed him into the room.

"*Veni, vidi, lunchi*," President Passant said. "We came, we saw, we ate split pea soup."

"May I ask a question, Mr. President?" Stanton said. "Why did we choose to speak to this small group, five days before the election?"

"What do you mean, Stanton? We speak to small groups all the time."

"Were these big donors, sir? They didn't look like big donors. They certainly didn't *smell* like big donors. But I have a more important question: why did you rile up a bunch of gun nuts and then give them the Democratic nominee's schedule? Or should I say, why did you just tell that militia group to gun down a fifteen-year-old boy?"

President Passant's smirk deepened. "That's ridiculous, Stanton. I simply meant they should vote for me, to keep the liberals from taking their guns."

The conflagration began in Stanton's stomach, flowed through his chest and down his arms, up his neck and cheeks, and finally inflamed his brain. It didn't come out as hot rage, Stanton was way past that. It came out as cold, soundless fury, barely above a whisper.

"That's it, Mr. President. You've crossed the line. Frankly, you crossed it a long time ago. I can't tell you how long I've wanted to do this, but I'm done. I quit." He stared into Passant's soulless eyes. "And I'm going to tell the world about you."

"I don't think so," Passant said.

"Really? Who's going to stop me?"

"Maryanne."

"What?"

Something hard and bulky slammed into the side of Stanton's head. He heard a hollow ringing, saw red and white sparks.

Then everything went black.

Forty-two

The next afternoon, at exactly 4:30pm, Paul and Sylvia exited the school to wait for their Secret Service agents to drive them to the venue of the bipartisan dinner. Mr. Creed had rented clothes for them and said they could change into them at the hotel. Paul wasn't crazy about wearing suits, much less tuxedoes, but the idea of seeing Sylvia in a fancy dress made his stomach tingle a little bit. As he did every time he went outside these days, he took his prop glasses from his backpack and slid them onto his face.

"You know, I really like those on you," Sylvia said. "They make you look cute."

Paul's stomach tingled again.

They continued discussing the Presidential Succession Act, which had been the topic of the day in AP American History, eighth period.

"So, after the Speaker of the House and the President *pro tem* of the Senate, they go through the Cabinet, right?" Paul said.

"Yeah," Sylvia said. "But I wonder why the Secretary of Homeland Security is last. If the top five or six guys in succession have been taken out, wouldn't Homeland Security be kind of important?"

"Certainly more important than having the Secretary of Agriculture so high on the list. How's he going to stem the national emergency? Plant some soybeans?"

Sylvia's giggle was like a small silver chime. Paul could have stood there listening to her giggle for hours. He tried to think of something else he could say to make her do it again, but she spoke first. "It's kind of fascinating," she said. "Considering the Speaker is in charge right now. It's like life imitating Civics class."

The Secret Service car drove up and two men got out, wearing the same dark suits all the Secret Service agents did, except these guys' clothes didn't fit. Especially the big one — taller even than John 86, but not quite as beefy — who wore flood pants and whose sleeves were at least four inches too short.

"You're not our usual guys," Paul said.

"No," the tall one said. "They got tied up."

They had the same dark sunglasses all the agents had, and the same curly wire things in their ears. Their ID pictures weren't perfect, but close enough, assuming the pictures were a couple years old, plus Paul knew from a series of disastrous school yearbook photos that head shots didn't always look like you hoped.

He and Sylvia climbed into the car.

The agents put their heads together in the front seat, seemingly discussing the best route to their destination. Paul and Sylvia looked at each other. Paul pulled up the map app on his phone and keyed in the Sofitel Hotel in Center City, Philadelphia.

Turn left on Montgomery Avenue, Siri said.

185

The driver turned right.

"I think the city is back behind us," Paul said.

"Don't worry," the driver said. "We know a better way."

Head west on Montgomery Avenue.

In a quarter mile, turn right onto Llanfair Road, then turn right onto Roberts Road.

Sylvia raised one eyebrow. They both knew what a "turn around" suggestion from Siri sounded like.

Turn right on Llanfair Road.

"You drove right past," Paul said. "You probably ought to listen to Siri. She usually knows what she's talking about."

"Relax, we're taking a short cut."

"More like a you-don't-know-where-the-hell-you're-going cut," Paul muttered to Sylvia. She giggled again.

They approached the Suburban Square shopping plaza, home of the Apple Store and the store where Paul's Mom sometimes took him to buy dreadful button-down shirts he refused to wear in public. Definitely the opposite direction from Center City.

In half a mile, turn left onto Anderson Road.

Turn left onto Anderson Road.

Turn left.

Now, Paul felt a lead ball in his stomach. He liked the tingly feeling better. "I may have zoned out for a moment in class," he said. "Is there some sort of *Candidate* Succession Act?"

Sylvia bit her lip. She took out her phone but before she could put it to her ear, the tall Secret Service agent turned in his seat. He didn't speak or even smile. He just stared at them as if they were mildly interesting specimens on the dissecting table.

Turn right onto Mill Creek Road.

Turn right.

In five hundred feet, make a U-turn.

Make a U-turn.

Make a U-turn.

Paul looked at Sylvia again. "Does Siri sound angrier to you?"

Forty-three

Kayla milled about the crowded press area two doors down from main hall where the bipartisan dinner had been set. She stopped near a large group containing her friend Andrea Robinson and CNN's Henderson Hooper.

Hooper was saying, "Word is, in addition to inappropriate jokes and awkward insults, Passant's going to unveil a new policy initiative tonight. Something all these swing state Pennsylvanians are going to love."

"Don't tell me," Andrea said. "He's going to build a wall over the Delaware River and make New Jersey pay for it?"

"More likely, he wants to repeal that Constitutional Amendment he stuffed down everybody's throat, three months ago," Hooper said. "Without that, he wouldn't be in the fix he is today, would he? Careful what you wish for, Mr. Passant." He laughed, then noticed Kayla. "And who would know better than the Democratic nominee's personal reporter. Where's your boy, Schwarzenegger?"

"No idea," Kayla said before anybody could ask if she was related to Arnold. "Excuse me while I find out." She wended her way through the journalists to find Lincoln Creed.

She passed Edward Passant, who seemed happier than he had in months, stalking through the press room wearing that stern expression he thought looked authoritative but at best looked predatory and more often, constipated. He shook every hand he could find, always hanging on a couple beats too long to the female ones. Kayla avoided him.

She found Creed inside the main ballroom, alternating his gaze between his watch and the entrance.

"Where are your candidates?" she said.

Creed acknowledged her briefly before looking at his watch again. "Damned if I know. But I hope to hell they get here soon. They're not picking up their phones and they haven't changed into their clothes yet."

He turned back to the entrance as if he could make the kids materialize out of thin air if only he stared hard enough. "Last thing we need is that boy taking the stage on national TV wearing a chess club hoodie."

*   *   *

Heath, dressed in the way-too-small suit he'd appropriated from the now-unconscious Secret Service agent, stood near the Colonel in a warehouse out in a place called King of Prussia, forty minutes west of the city of Philadelphia. He wiggled his toes. The clothes were uncomfortable but at least he had his own shoes. No way he could have fit into the agent's footwear. They'd left them behind, tossed behind a hedge on the side of the school where hopefully nobody would find them.

The Colonel gave orders. The prisoners were securely bound and dumped on the floor near the wall. Guns were unpacked and loaded. Militiamen deployed themselves. Heath took in everything with painstaking care, watching, listening, evaluating.

He didn't like what he was hearing.

"OK, I understand why we're against blacks, Muslims, and Mexicans," he said. "I guess. But tell me again what we have against children?"

"You heard the President," the Colonel said. "We have to act to preserve our liberty and freedoms. The boy threatens our way of life."

Heath examined their teenaged prisoners, at least one of whom he'd admired from afar. He remembered seeing Paul Urbina-Pedisich speak on TV and liking what he heard. He watched several LCPVM members pointing automatic weapons at the kids, clearly depriving their prisoners of liberty and freedom in a significantly more profound way than any "anti-gun" judge ever could. He wondered why some people's liberty and freedoms were more important than other's. He wondered if anybody had thought to bring supper. His gaze wandered around the warehouse.

"Who's that guy over in the corner?" He pointed at a man standing apart from the group. The man had a ruddy, stubbled face and was shrouded in shadow, though it was unclear what interrupted light source caused the darkness around him. Heath thought he recognized him but couldn't place from where.

"Some White House bigwig," the Colonel said. "He arranged the warehouse and also, the General told me this morning, a large honorarium to the LCPVM discretionary account. Works direct for the President, I hear. I mean President Passant, of course."

Yes, that's where Heath had seen the man. On the news. His name was Stew Cannon and other than President Passant's relatives, he was his closest advisor.

The others listened to the Colonel and took his information as a sign that their actions were pre-ordained. Or, at least approved and actively encouraged by as high up as you could get in the mortal world. Heath took a different view.

"So, does that make us freedom fighters, or hit men?"

His fiancé kept her AK-47 trained on the little girl.

"Shut up, honey," she said.

Forty-four

A boy wearing a chess club hoodie appeared in the ballroom entrance, but it wasn't Paul Urbina-Pedisich. Kayla recognized Artie, the keeper of the octopus, flanked by two very large boys wearing football jerseys.

Artie saw Kayla and ran toward her, with the large boys close behind. "We've been looking all over," the boy said. "We couldn't find you anywhere."

"Well, you've found me now," Kayla said. "What is it, something happened to Orville?"

"Way worse than that," Artie said. "We think something's happened to Paul and Sylvia. Neither of them is answering their phones, and we found these behind the bushes."

The large African-American boy wearing number 86 held up a pair of black shoes, of the sort favored by the Secret Service.

Creed examined the shoes, found a name tag that matched one of the agents assigned to Paul. He beckoned over an agent who stood by the doorway.

"Trouble," he said.

A few minutes later, they convened in the kitchen. The catering staff was cleared out. Creed joined the Secret Service Special Agent in Charge and the head of Passant's private security team, a burly man with a thinning hairline and only nine fingers. Kayla tagged along, ostensibly as the adult responsible for the boys, hoping nobody would notice she didn't belong.

The boys told their story again. They handed over the footwear. The Special Agent studied the shoes then stepped away to contact his superiors.

Fifteen minutes later he returned to the group. "Yeah, we found them, the entire detail. They were jumped from behind and knocked out, trussed up and left in the back of an SUV registered to some militia group in Central PA. The threats took car keys, IDs, and uniforms. The protectees probably got in the car willingly."

His eyes were red with self-recrimination, like he wanted to lock himself up. "They could be a hundred fifty miles away by now and we have no idea where to look."

Creed reached into his pocket for his phone. "That's not entirely true, Special Agent."

"What do you mean?"

"I got three teenage nephews. I know how hard they are to keep track of, always off sniffing the roses, or other sweet things. Didn't want that to happen with the Democratic nominee for President of the United States. My job's hard enough as it is." He turned to Kayla and winked. "So I stuck a GPS tracker on his eyeglasses."

He held up his phone. "Looks like they're out by the King of Prussia Mall."

"The kids went to the *mall?*" Kayla said.

Creed frowned. "Doubt it."

The Secret Service man snatched Creed's phone, input the GPS coordinates into his own device. "Looks like a large building, possibly a warehouse. I'll need to keep this in case they go on the move," he said. "Problem is, this could be some sort of coordinated attack. Assuming it's a kidnap situation, I don't have enough agents on hand to overwhelm a hostile force entrenched in a warehouse while also keeping a reasonable force here to guard my other protectee."

"We can take care of President Passant," the nine-fingered private security guy said.

"That's debatable," the Special Agent said. "And I don't have time to debate. I will not abandon a protectee under any circumstances."

"I'm not the one who lost two of my charges," Nine Fingers said. "But fine, I'll bring half my force to supplement yours in the field, help you out of your embarrassing mess." He smirked at his counterpart. "Unless you want to just stay here? Leave your little sheep alone, and hope they come home, wagging their tails behind them?"

The Special Agent returned the security man's stare and growled under his breath. Finally, he gave a single, curt nod.

"Let's go, people," he said, waving for a squad of agents to join him. "I've never lost a protectee and I don't intend to start now."

They whisked away, leaving Kayla, Creed, and the three boys standing alone in the kitchen. Creed watched the agents leave with a deep frown on his face.

"What is it?" Kayla said.

"Election's in four days. No chance to get ourselves another candidate. Anything happens, Passant wins by default."

Kayla held her one hand with the other to keep from smacking the old man. "*That's* what you're worried about?"

"You want another three years of Mr. Instability? No accounting for taste." He raised an eyebrow. "But that's not what I meant."

"What, then?"

"Passant would know that too, that he'd win by default. And he's never been particularly fond of our boy, has he?"

Kayla gasped. "And we just sent Passant's own private security force out there." She grabbed Creed's shoulders. "Tell me you copied down the address of that warehouse."

Creed chuckled. "Naturally."

"Then what are we waiting for?" the football players said in unison. "Let's go!"

Forty-five

Paul was only 15, but he could recognize "counter-intelligence" when he saw it. These jokers may have had enough weapons to fight a war with Serbia, but they needed all that firepower to compensate for a distinct deficiency upstairs.

For one thing, they hadn't thought to gag either Paul or Sylvia. Not that shouting in an abandoned warehouse would have done either kid much good, but if you're going to make the effort of kidnapping someone and tying them up, why not go all the way? For that matter — pro tip — if you plan to tie somebody up, best to invest in a box of zip ties, rather than resort to a bunch of jumbled, smartphone charger cords.

Better was the guy who kept asking why there was a *King* of Prussia in the United States of *America*, who in addition to not getting that people were different from places, committed the bad guy *faux pas* of telling his hostages exactly where they'd been taken. Best of all, in a morbid, I'm-probably-going-to-die-in-ten-minutes-anyway sort of way, was the argument over which weapon provided the most "patriotic" method of murdering a couple of unarmed children.

The guy in charge argued in favor of a single shot to the heart from an old handgun that had once belonged to his father's father, while others wanted to go even further and employ an antique musket that probably hadn't been fired since 1768. The woman pointing a really big gun at Sylvia suggested they use whatever fired the most rounds per minute, to make sure they didn't miss their bound, unmoving targets. But the consensus seemed to center on the big ol' bazooka somebody had brought with them, until someone else pointed out the local police might get interested if the geniuses blew out the back wall of the building.

The only exception to the rampant stupidity virus was the big one, although he was still wearing the flood pants and short sleeve jacket. Aside from that, he actually seemed pretty smart, long as you didn't object to driving 25 in a 60 mph zone. And he didn't seem totally and mindlessly committed to the cause, either.

Paul directed his efforts at him.

"I don't know why you're doing this, but think about it. We're children. Just because we're running for office doesn't mean we deserve to die."

The man looked straight at Paul. His eyes were big and brown and kind. And a little sad. He glanced around at all the fanatical faces, teeth bared and weapons raised. His own gun was holstered. He sighed but didn't say anything.

"Please," Paul said, in his youngest-sounding, most frightened voice — which, frankly, didn't require even a little bit of acting. "You seem like a good guy, so you know this is wrong. You're not much older than we are. We have our whole lives ahead of us. Don't do this."

"Enough already!" the guy in charge said. He pointed his father's father's pistol straight at Paul's heart.

"I'm so sorry," Paul said to Sylvia. "This is all my fault. If I hadn't picked you as my Vice President, you wouldn't be here now. You wouldn't—"

Sylvia shut him up by shimmying next to him and kissing him right on the mouth.

For a moment, his breath got knocked out of him and he just sat there, stunned. But almost immediately he recovered and returned her kiss, actively and fervently and reverently as if it were the last thing he'd ever do, which there was a pretty good chance it was. He tasted her lips, her tongue tickled his. Soft and wet and wonderful. He wouldn't have traded that moment for anything.

Even if they were both about to die.

Forty-six

"Enough already!"

Heath watched the Colonel aim his grandfather's gun at Paul Urbina-Pedisich's chest, but he didn't fire because even the Colonel wouldn't shoot two people who were kissing. Well, maybe he would if one of them was his daughter, but as far as Heath knew, Sylvia Humphries wasn't even a cousin.

He knew he shouldn't think of them as Paul and Sylvia, like when he'd named that turtle he'd found in the woods and it died three days later. But he'd seen so much of them on TV and the computer news that he almost felt he knew them.

And he was sure Paul was looking at him when he'd spoken a minute earlier, sure that he'd spoken to *him*, as if Heath mattered, and wasn't just a slow foot soldier in a war that had been fought and lost in 1865 and 1954 and 1964. Besides, he thought the kissing was kind of sweet, he kind of wished he was kissing his fiancé at that moment and not preparing to witness an execution. He looked around for his fiancé, maybe to blow her an air kiss, but she was too busy breaking up the prisoners and waving for the Colonel to get it over with.

An unpleasant grin crossed the Colonel's face. "Time to finish this filthy Mexican."

"Stop!" Paul struggled to his feet. Everybody gaped at him. "I'm not Mexican, not that there'd be anything wrong with it if I was. My great-grandfather immigrated here from Spain, which makes me one-eighth Spanish. You see, I'm really into my family tree, that's how I know I'm also one-quarter Lithuanian Jewish—"

"A Jew!" The Colonel snarled.

"—and one-eighth Polish Catholic and one-sixteenth Dutch-turned-Mormon. I'm one-eighth Irish and one-eighth French—"

"A Frenchy?" someone said from the back. "So he *is* connected to ISIS!"

"—plus one-sixteenth each, Australian, Japanese, and Navajo Indian. That's why my Twitter handle is @MeltingPUP, I'm a little bit of everything." The boy tried to take a step forward but with his feet bound, he only stumbled to his knees.

"Don't you see?" Paul said. "That's what being American is in the Twenty-First Century. We're *all* a little bit of everything. Even if your ancestors came from just one country, we all live here now. There's no reason for hate."

"Nice speech," the Colonel said while most of the room hooted and hollered. "Now, don't move."

"Wait," Heath said. "Paul's right. They're *children*. Our patriotic duty can't possibly involve slaughtering our youth." He stepped forward, within arm's reach of the Colonel. "Please, sir, you don't have to do this."

The Colonel snorted. "Yes, I do." He straightened his arm and curved his finger.

"No." Heath unholstered his own gun, more quickly than he'd ever done anything in his life, and pressed the muzzle against the Colonel's right temple. "You don't."

He smiled at Paul and nodded. He smiled at Sylvia.

He heard the bolt of an assault rifle slap into place. Right behind him.

He turned his head. His fiancé's AK-47 was aimed at the center of his back.

His own beloved. Heath's heart sank in his chest, his eyes welled. He barely noticed the other two other LCPVM "patriots" who had stepped up and trained their weapons on him. Only his ruptured love mattered. He dropped his gun and raised both arms in surrender.

The Colonel sneered. "We'll deal with you later." He straightened his arm again.

He yelped. His gun went flying out of his hand, which bloomed crimson like time-lapse photography of a pure red rose coming open in the springtime. The Colonel hopped and yammered then went down to the floor as if someone had hit him with an invisible two-by-four.

Heath stared while the Colonel clutched at his knee and howled at the universe. He watched the exact same thing happen to his fiancé's hand and gun and knee. Then to one of the others. Heath swung his head wildly from side to side.

He couldn't tell where the attack was coming from.

Forty-seven

Seamus took out the fourth gunman. All four of them writhed on the ground, clutching their shattered knees with their wounded hands. Seamus watched them thrash and groan from his vantage on the ceiling-level catwalk.

The others scattered. They loved their guns, but no matter what they said on Facebook, none of them actually liked weapons enough to risk being shot or killed by one.

He looked around to make sure the immediate danger had passed. The only one still standing was the tall one, but he'd already discarded his weapon and raised his hands. Also, Passant's shadowy advisor, off in the corner, but he wasn't armed. It was safe to go down and finish the job.

He reached the floor and took his ear buds out for a moment. He wanted to hear what the kid had to say for himself.

"You!" the boy said. "You're the assassin who tried to kill me in New York, aren't you?"

Seamus bared his teeth. "I suspected the President would make another move. I've been watching, waiting, ready to step in when he did. When I heard about the bipartisan dinner, I knew the timing was right. He couldn't wait any longer. But I wasn't going let it happen that way, I had my own task to complete.

The boy swallowed. "To kill me yourself?"

Seamus chuckled. He looked at the gun in his hand. "'Course not," he said. "To keep Passant from doing it." He began to pace. "I should have said no the first time, should have known it wasn't a national security issue. Can't fix that, but you have to look forward, I always say."

He put his ear buds back in. "Besides, I'd never shoot you, I owe you everything. When I read all that stuff about you and Justin Bieber, I got curious and downloaded a few of his songs. It's *exactly* what I needed. I'll never fall asleep on the job again."

Paul raised both arms to the heavens. "For the last time, I DO *NOT* LISTEN TO JUSTIN BIEBER. Why won't anybody *listen* to me?"

Seamus took his ear buds back out for a second. "Sorry, I missed that. Did you say something?"

Two dozen men in black suits burst into the warehouse. "Nobody move. Everyone lay your weapons on the floor." The cavalry had finally come.

Seamus did as he was told. The suits relaxed their own weapons, though they all still gripped them in their hands.

The newcomers were split evenly between Secret Service and Passant private security. They seemed paired together, one of each, probably the Service's idea to keep the cowboys in line. No, not totally even, there was one unpaired security guy. Seamus recognized the balding, nine-fingered guard who'd let him in to Passant Place during the gig in New York.

Nine Fingers swaggered up to him, gun drawn. "Seamus Callahan, as I live and breathe. What a lovely surprise." He cocked his weapon. "You've been on my list for quite a while."

"Wait!" the kid said. "You got it all wrong. He *saved* us. He's one of the good guys."

Nine Fingers made a motion with his off hand. The private security guys all turned on their partners, guns up and ready. The betrayal caught the agents off guard, none of them had their weapons in position to strike back. Stunned silence filled the warehouse.

The Agent in Charge made his play. He chopped out with his left hand while his right raised his gun.

His "partner" was ready. He countered the blow and cold-cocked the agent, who collapsed in a heap. The other agents watched, with sullen expressions. None of them handed over their weapons, but none of them made a move, either.

"No." Nine Fingers smiled at the kid. "I got it right."

He aimed at Seamus's head. "First the traitor, then the two little threats." His finger tightened against the trigger.

Something large hurtled into Nine Fingers from behind. His gun went flying amidst the thud of bodies smashing and the crunch of ribs snapping. The security man's head hit the cement floor with a sickening crunch.

A gigantic African-American boy got up and roared over his victim. He made the strong man gesture with both arms. "I just live for the big hits," he said.

Forty-eight

Paul blinked. John 86? What was he doing here? The private security gang seemed stunned as well. The Secret Service guys took advantage, and within a few minutes the bad guys had all been trussed up and marched outside.

He heard John 69's voice, too. "Hold it right there," he said to President Passant's advisor, who was attempting to tiptoe out a rear exit. "Unless you want the same treatment."

Stew Cannon took one look at the unconscious body of Nine Fingers, limbs sprawled in several unnatural directions, and promptly surrendered.

The big militiaman bent down to assist the woman who'd held them captive. He wrapped his arm around her shoulders while she limped and whimpered.

"Dearest," the big man said. "I hope you don't get cross with me, but I don't think I want to get married any more. We're just not right for each other."

The assassin smiled. He pulled a jagged knife from his waistband. His eyes shone with intensity as he advanced on Paul and Sylvia. Paul gasped, tried to shield Sylvia with his body.

The guy smiled. The light glinted off one of his front teeth. He placed a hand on Paul's shoulder, pinned him against the wall. He bent down, brandished the knife. When he cut through the jumbled cords binding their wrists and ankles, Paul let out a humongous sigh.

The Agent in Charge regained consciousness. He struggled to his feet, surveyed the situation.

"I'm sure as hell not looking forward to writing *this* report," he said.

*   *   *

Paul and Sylvia spent the weekend at home, recuperating. Mr. Creed said it was OK because every news story was about the kidnapping anyway, so it wasn't like they were out of the news cycle. President Passant tweeted that the Secret Service was incompetent and that Paul and Sylvia had never been in any real danger, stating unequivocally that the kidnapping had been a clever misdirection and that *he* had been the actual assassination target.

CNN ran a big segment on Henderson Hooper 180. The two Republicans on the panel said they feared for President Passant's safety. The others on the panel said they feared for their two colleagues' sanity. Sam Hattery on Fox News, citing several unsourced accounts by "ever vigilant" right wing media outlets, insisted the attempt on Passant's life was the first step in a far-reaching plot to seize power on the part of Alison Denton, the Democratic National Committee, Paul's Mom, and gay members of the Boy Scouts of America. A DNC spokesperson denied having any connection to the Boy Scouts.

Mr. Creed said none of it mattered. Passant had once again changed the subject. Whatever political gains Paul had garnered from his ordeal had floated away on the breeze. They were back to square one.

School on Monday was a blur. Paul seemed to remember a great deal of hugging and back-slapping and high-fiving, but little else. After the final bell, his usual Secret Service guys, wearing new suits and sheepish expressions, picked him and Sylvia up and drove them to campaign headquarters, where they did a couple live interviews and then went home again.

Dinner with his family was a quiet affair. His parents kept looking at him with sad, anxious smiles. Even his brother behaved himself.

Paul slept very little that night. He couldn't wait for it all to be over.

Forty-nine

School was off on Election Day. Paul spent the day locked inside campaign headquarters because Mr. Creed didn't want to risk him accidentally screwing anything up.

"Nothing more we can do," Mr. Creed said. "If the youth vote turns out, we have a pretty fair chance to win. If they don't, just butter us up and pop us in the toaster."

Paul passed most of the afternoon closeted with his running mate in a small office. He had hoped maybe they could make out again, but she said she was too nervous. At 6pm, a staffer brought them clothes, the same tux and long dress he and Sylvia were supposed to have worn at the bipartisan dinner. They put on their costumes and drove with Kayla and Mr. Creed to the same ballroom at the Sofitel Hotel, for the big Democratic Election Day gala.

The room was all made up with banners and red-white-and-blue streamers. Huge TVs were set up all over, including one that took up a whole wall on one side. Flanking the stage were twenty-foot high pictures of Paul and Sylvia. A dozen bands played 45 minutes each. When Justin Bieber took the stage, Paul stuck his fingers in his ears and shouted, "Nah, nah, nah, nah," for the entire performance.

By 11pm, Paul had won New York, Connecticut, Delaware and Rhode Island, and lost Alabama, Mississippi, Tennessee, and West Virginia. In other words, nothing Mr. Creed hadn't told him weeks ago. Andrea Robinson on the big TV was about to call New Jersey when someone put their hand on Paul's shoulder.

He turned. "Oh, hi Mom."

"I think it's time to go home," she said. "You have school tomorrow."

Paul looked up at her and shuddered. "What if I don't?"

She patted him on the head. "If you think becoming President of the United States will allow you to skip school for the next three years, you have another thing coming, young man."

"That's not what I meant."

"I know."

"Seriously, Mom. This is all so crazy. We've all been talking about what if we lose, but what if we *win*? What will I do then?"

"You'll do your best. I know you will."

She pulled him close and gave him a big hug. He felt warm and happy and safe, for the first time in ages. He even forgot to be embarrassed about his mother embracing him right there, in front of everybody.

"Don't worry, Paul," she said. "You'll always have me and your father, no matter what. We'll always be there for you. Your brother too."

"Now, why'd you have to go and spoil it?" Paul said.

She put her arm around his shoulder. "Come on home, honey. It's bedtime."

*   *   *

Just before midnight on Election Day, they found Stanton Young, bound, gagged, and naked, in the basement of a hookah lounge outside Baltimore, Maryland. They took him to the nearest trauma ward, gave him a hospital gown and a hot meal, and advised him not to agitate himself.

The police attempted to question him, but all they could get out of him was, "Youth turnout, what's the youth turnout," over and over. The officers concluded he'd been a participant in a kinky sex-game gone terribly wrong, and declined to file a police report.

*   *   *

The sun poured through the blinds in Paul's bedroom the next day. He'd been dreaming about something, but couldn't remember any of it. He rolled out of bed, showered, and traipsed down to the kitchen for breakfast.

Mr. Creed stood by the refrigerator, quietly talking to Kayla. Both wore grim expressions. Kayla noticed Paul and gestured toward him with her chin. Mr. Creed turned and started to speak but then ran his hand over his jowls and said nothing.

Sylvia was there, too. Soon as Paul met her eyes, she launched herself at him, threw her arms around his neck, and burst into tears.

His parents both seemed a little weepy, too. Paul's shoulders slumped. He let out a big sigh. He would never admit it, but a big part of him was relieved, almost happy. He felt a hundred pounds lighter.

"Oh well, we tried, right?" he said.

Mr. Creed came over and laid his hand on Paul's shoulder.

"Mr. President, would you like to watch Edward Passant's concession speech?"

Paul's insides went entirely numb. His hands shook uncontrollably. He had to grab on to the counter to keep from falling over.

"WHAT?!?"

"They're calling it the 'Youth Revolution,'" Mr. Creed said. "Biggest young voter turnout ever. We won states the Democrats hadn't carried in forty years. Four-hundred-forty electoral votes to ninety-eight, twentieth biggest electoral margin in history."

He picked up the remote, powered up the TV, switched the channel to MSNBC. The numbers "440" and "98" were plastered in the upper right corner of the screen. The panelists were arguing whether or not the voters had given President Urbina-Pedisich a "mandate."

The host said, "All right, hold that thought. Now let's go, live, to Passant Place, where Edward N. Passant is about to formally concede."

President Passant thanked his supporters, his family and, most of all, himself.

"I actually won this election," he said. "If not for the eighty-eight million votes that were cast illegally. That's right, people. Eighty-eight million. You know how I know those votes were fraudulent? Because they weren't for me."

"At least he concedes a million and a half of your votes were legit," Mr. Creed said.

Sylvia came over and gave Paul another hug, then leaned in and gave him a kiss, right on the lips. Paul's parents looked at each other and smiled, seemingly a lot happier about that than about Paul winning the election.

"Are we done watching television?" Paul's Mom said. "The bus is going to be here in two minutes."

Fifty

Paul Urbina-Pedisich was sworn in as the 47th President of the United States on January 20, 2018. Due to the shortened transition period, the new Administration hadn't yet filled all the Cabinet level or even West Wing positions, but one of the first appointments was Kayla Schwarzenegger as White House Press Secretary.

Kayla leaned on a desk in the outer office area in front of the Oval, waiting for Lincoln Creed to get off the phone.

"Great, thanks," he said before he disconnected the call. "All right, Alison Denton has finally agreed to come on as Chief of Staff. We're almost there."

"You didn't want that job, yourself? After you did this amazing thing?"

He leaned back and rocked in his chair. "Nah. Never been an ambition of mine, to keep the streets clean. Besides, I have to worry about the next guy."

Kayla noticed Stanton Young on the television, giving an interview outside a Federal courthouse. She turned up the volume.

"It gives me no pleasure to announce Mr. Passant's arraignment on fourteen counts of assault, kidnapping, inciting a felony, and attempted murder," he said. "But under the circumstances, I felt testifying was the right thing to do."

He wasn't the only one. Once Stew Cannon realized the election was lost and there'd be no presidential pardon waiting for him, he flipped faster than you can say "minimum security prison." He knew most of the bankers in there, anyway. Between his testimony, Stanton's, and the nine-fingered security chief's, a Passant indictment seemed inevitable.

The screen shifted to a live interview with Edward Passant. "Nobody cares about attempted homicides, OK? Nobody. The only people who care are you fake media types. You're still trying to job me out of an election."

"An election you lost?" the interviewer said.

"See, there you go again. The election was rigged. Everyone knows it. Eighty-eight million fraudulent votes, that's a well-documented alternative fact."

Passant went on to announce the formation of a legal "platoon" to defend him against the unjust murder accusations. CNN's legal experts, who had studied all the facts, alternative facts, statements, and pleadings in the matter, conservatively predicted the case would get to trial in approximately 32 years.

Much more imminent was the sexual assault and harassment lawsuit. After Kayla's article, so many women had surfaced to press charges against Passant that they made the thing into a class action suit. Kayla, herself, was plaintiff number 414, but she was much happier about plaintiff number one, the named plaintiff in the lawsuit, Stephanie Wood, Stanton's former aide. Legal experts suggested this suit would cost the former President hundreds of millions, primarily because his defense on every one of the 492 counts appeared to be, "Look at her. No way!"

The President and Vice President of the United States entered the outer office, followed by a group of new Secret Service recruits. Two of those were the young football players who had helped foil the assassination plot, both of whom had arranged to graduate high school a few months early and agreed to wear pants for the duration of their tenure in the Service. The third was a former member of the Lycoming County Pennsylvania Volunteer Militia named Heath Dunbar, who had signed up the very day the President-Elect's testimony had cleared both him and new Director of Clandestine Services Seamus Callahan.

Kayla had bumped into Heath several times in the past couple weeks. He looked a lot more handsome when he wore clothes that fit. He seemed thoughtful and kind and surprisingly contemplative. Kayla wondered whether his deliberate manner might be an interesting counterpoint to her constant rapidity. She also wondered whether he'd ever muster the courage to ask her out, or if she'd have to ask him.

Vice President Humphries noticed the large aquarium on the opposite wall. She turned to the President. "You brought Orville the Octopus?"

"They said I could," said President Urbina-Pedisich. "But with his forty million Twitter followers, how could they say no? They won't let me make him Director of Fish and Wildlife, though. Maybe we'll give that one to Artie."

"Didn't you promise the people you'd appoint qualified officials?"

"Yeah, but looking back historically, I'm not sure how much that matters. Hey, you want to see the Oval Office?"

The Vice President giggled, encouraging the President's smile to widen even further. "So, you remember in American History when we talked about the Twenty-Fifth Amendment?" he said to her. "It says if I feel like it, I can step down temporarily from being President, even just for a day. So, if you want to be the very first female President, we can do that, like, for your birthday or something."

"That's so sweet!" She reached out her tiny little hand and placed it inside his as they entered the Oval Office.

"Ooh," the President said. "Tomorrow, you want to go with me to see the FBI Director and find out if there really are X-Files?"

The door closed behind them.

"Yep," Creed said. "I got to worry about the next guy. Republicans already have the little brother on retainer. Over/under on impeachment proceedings is Memorial Day. Then — fun, fun, fun — we get to do this all over again."

Kayla patted the stack of legal tender in her pocket, courtesy of Benny Bagodonuts and 3-to-2 odds. Memorial Day, eh? She liked their chances for the "over." She sat down and stretched her arms over her head. "We can enjoy today, though, right?"

"You bet," Creed said.

"I don't know what you could do for an encore." She gestured toward the closed Oval Office door and the children cavorting behind it. "What could possibly top this on the public's something-different meter?"

"No idea," he said. "Like you say, that's for tomorrow. Tonight, I'm sitting back, watching a ballgame, and pouring myself a nice, stiff drink."

But he didn't get out of his chair. His brow furrowed.

His gaze lingered on the octopus.

DEDICATION

In memory of two people I wish were around to read this book:

Jeff Kedson, who if he were alive today would either be in Washington, DC, fighting against the White House, or in some foreign country, as far from the White House as he could possibly get;

Bobbie Shaid, who if she were alive today would be forcing all her friends and acquaintances to buy this book.

ABOUT THE AUTHOR

David Kedson graduated from Duke University and the University of Pennsylvania Law School, after which he bounced around the usual hodgepodge of dead-end occupations — litigation attorney, entrepreneur, CEO, computer programmer, independent stock trader, and stay-at-home dad (which was by far the most challenging and most rewarding). These days, when he isn't spending time as a committee person for the local Democratic Committee, he sits around and makes things up. In his spare time, he cracks jokes.

ACKNOWLEDGMENTS

To my wonderful wife, Susan, who allows me to spend my time writing things (one of the many reasons why I love her);

To my son, Brandon, who inspires me every day, at least when he isn't too busy being a teenager;

To my Mom and Dad (Phyllis and Len), who despite not agreeing with me politically, have always done everything they could possibly do to encourage me and be great parents;

To Jessica Jaffe, for her fabulous cover design;

And to my agent, Janet Reid, who probably doesn't want her name associated with this project in any way, but is going to have to live with it.

Made in the USA
Middletown, DE
13 August 2017